The Dreams of

Sqwal's Deep

M.P. Foxx

Published by YouWriteOn.com, 2010
Copyright © M.P. Foxx
First Edition

A CIP catalogue record for this title is available from the British Library.

To my Daddy.

His grace is indescribable
His love is immeasurable
His mercy is unstoppable
His life is undeniable

Do you know Him?

Other books by M.P. Foxx

Wyldewych

1

The Fallen Two

Magh paced the outside of the clearing, looking passed the stone markers to where the moon cast shadows in the forest.

A fire burned bright and hot in the middle of the clearing. Behind one of the seven stone markers seven creatures, neither human nor animal, huddled together. She watched them, disgust etched on her face. Then tree tops swayed in the distance.

'At last,' she said loudly, turning her attention away from the startled beasts. Ravens circled over head, a few swooping down to perch on the nearby trees.

The sound of twigs cracking under feet. From the shadows two figures emerged. Two men, a thick layer of dirt and ash covered their hands and masked their faces.

'You are certain it is gone?' She asked the man with curly black hair.

'Yes, everything has been destroyed. There is no sign of Er or his dog. Wyldewych is nothing but dust and ash.'

'And the tree?'

The man shook his head. 'A sapling grows in its place. As hard as I tried, I could not uproot it.'

Magh breathed in slowly, a frown etched across her face. She left the men and walked over to the huge pot that was sitting in the fire. 'You will not be able to. The tree has been reborn and evil cannot touch it. For now.'

She stared in to the fire, deep in thought. The man with the curly hair came up behind her.

'We believe that the boy has the Arcrux,' he said in a low voice.

She turned her head towards him. 'You have heard from Fury?'

'No,' the man hesitated. 'He has been unable to get past the door in the house.'

Magh shook her head and made a dismissive gesture with her hands. 'The boy has it, he must have it. That is why Fury cannot get back, nor should he dare come back without the Arcrux.' She circled the fire. 'No, the boy has it, I'm sure of it.' Her index finger tapped her chin. 'He must be stopped, but how?'

'If I can make a suggestion,' the man with the curly hair came around to her. Magh eyed him suspiciously. 'As you know, my brother has just been made lieutenant of-'

'This mission has been given to me, Emrel,' Magh shot back. 'And I, not your brother will see it through.' She fixed him with a steely look.

'As you wish,' Emrel bowed his head slightly and joined the other man in the shadows.

'No,' Magh continued. 'The boy cannot return to Meridia. But I cannot stop him, it has to be his choice to stay away, or I have failed. He knows what he must do here, even if it means his life. But he still chooses to accept it. Why?' Magh stared blankly for a moment, and then her face lit up.

'Because he feels his life is worth nothing now that he knows the truth about his parents.' Her eyes searched and then rested on the beasts across the fire. 'But what if his life outside of Meridia suddenly changed? What if he had – a distraction? Something to keep his mind off Meridia? Yes!' She strode towards the beasts. 'Something he desires more than anything else.' She stopped short of the beasts and grabbed two piles of dirt off the ground.

'Mange. Madame Heera.' Magh spoke loudly. The beasts stopped their snorting and all seven heads shot to attention. Two of the beasts slowly hobbled towards her.

The beast she called Mange came to her first. His long, skinny arms hung loosely beside his short, frog-like body. His long feet slapped against the ground as he walked. He was green from head to toe, save for his small white eyes and sparse, stringy grey hair. His thick tongue licked his six sharp teeth.

Magh glanced at him and winced before looking past him. 'Madame Heera, what are you waiting for?'

From behind Mange, Madame Heera hobbled up. Even with a huge hunch in her back, Mange only came up to her shoulders. Her curly brown hair clung in patches to her dry, flaky scalp. Her uneven legs caused her to limp towards her master, grey eyes looking timid, almost scared.

Magh looked back at her in disgust. 'You've seen better days.' She backed away from them, standing between them and the roaring fire. 'You know that you are in a lifetime of servitude to me.' Her words were met with shrieks of protest from the seven beasts.

Waiting for the noise to die down, she continued. 'There's no use moaning now, is there? You should have made different decisions all those years ago then, shouldn't you? Hm?' Her eyes went from Mange to Madame Heera. 'I would tell you what I'm about to do, but I can't stand to look at you a minute longer. So,' she bent down to them. 'This won't hurt a bit.' She threw the handfuls of dirt over them and called out a spell.

Desire and envy born from shame; the child's one wish shall it remain

After repeating it three times she picked up the two beasts and threw them in to the pot on the fire. Immediately they struggled and jerked in the pot as Magh looked on. The five remaining beasts screeched in surprise while the ravens squawked. The two men stood watching quietly in the shadows.

2

Fury

'Ow!' Dark red blood bubbled at the top of Benjamin's finger before trickling down the side of his hand.

From his kneeling position he sighed deeply, stood up and went to the kitchen sink behind him. Water, tinted blood red swirled down the drain. He looked out the window to the back garden. Snow had come the night before and covered the unruly landscape with a thick, white blanket. He turned the tap off and dried his finger, ready to face the mess he had waiting for him. Smashed glass sparkled against the dark tiles of the kitchen floor. Bending down to pick it up, he played it back in his mind, piecing together how it happened.

Catching a moment alone, he had went to get a drink of water before school, giving him an excuse to pass by and try the cellar door again. Standing in the kitchen, he watched the door handle intently as he sipped his water. It had been over a year since his return from Meridia, and now, five days before his twelfth birthday, he was starting to accept his grim reality. It was last year that the door handle to the cellar door began to shake, and when he put his hand on it that night it had swung open, hurtling him down the stairs and in to Meridia. Although scared at first, it had not taken him long to feel like he belonged there, and when he learned all about his parents and how they were killed, every question he ever had about them had been answered in that moment. It hadn't taken him long to get used to the fact that not only was Meridia in danger, but he was the only one that could help them. He was the only one, Gideon told him, who could fight off the evil that grew. Gideon, the wise old man he met in Meridia, had brought him back at the right time, he had said.

But now that he was back at Hadley Priest Children's Home, Benjamin had had his doubts. It had been so long since he had been back, it must have been a mistake. He knew it all along, it must have been a mix-up and Gideon had finally realised he had got the wrong person. By now Gideon had found the real person and *they* were going to save Meridia, not him. But how could Gideon have been so wrong?

His thoughts of Meridia brought him back to something all too familiar - his dreams. Before he had been haunted by dreams of a man with no face, and now other dreams disturbed his sleep as well. Only last night he had dreamt of two people by a fire, and talk of somebody called Fury. Was Fury was the faceless man in his other dreams? He fingered the stone in his pocket. Since Gideon gave it to him after raising the

11

oracle about himself at the Bogwumps, he never had it out of his reach. He closed his eyes until he could feel the weight of the Arcrux around his neck. The Arcrux that Gideon gave him to hold the leagues that would one day save Meridia. His thoughts made him dizzy and doubt crept in once more. And then it happened, or so he thought. As he opened his eyes towards the cellar door he was sure he saw the handle move.

Without looking, he had slammed his glass down, not making sure it was balanced. He was halfway to the door when he heard a pop behind him followed by bits of glass bouncing across tile. He jumped and turned briefly before continuing towards the door, towards freedom.

He gripped the handle, confident this time. Over the past year he would try it half-heartedly, when he knew no one was around but it never moved. But this time was different, he could feel it. He tugged on the handle – nothing. He tried again, but the door was as it always was, shut tight. He turned to the portrait of Hadley Priest hanging on the opposite wall.

'I suppose you're going to tell me I just imagined everything, like you never spoke to me that time.' He examined every brush stroke of the old oil painting, the man in the portrait as stiff as a statue.

'Stupid painting,' he turned around and glared at the door. 'Stupid door,' his voice hardened.

Shards of glass sparkled against the kitchen floor. 'Stupid glass.' Picking the larger bits up with his hands while glancing up at the door left an opportunity for him to cut himself.

He shook his head slightly, concentrating on what he was doing. He realised now what had happened, his own eagerness had got the best of him. Feeling ridiculous, Benjamin carefully cradled the smaller bits of glass in his hand before dropping them gently in to the bin. He stifled a groan at the sound of Hester's bedroom door opening.

'What do you think you're doing?' Hester strode out. 'I'm trying to sleep.' Not even the sight of Hester in curlers and a dressing gown could make Benjamin smile. 'And what's all this?' She motioned to the broken glass.

'I dropped a glass,' Benjamin's eyes never left the floor. 'I wasn't thinking, I'm sorry.'

Hester's hands found her hips. 'I'll say. Not thinking is just the beginning. Stupid boy.'

Benjamin stopped what he was doing and let an awkward silence pass. 'I said I was sorry.'

A rumble of feet coming downstairs and the presence of Marcus and Riley broke the tension.

Hester recoiled. 'Well, just make sure you get it all cleaned up. If I get glass in my feet, you'll wish you were never born.'

13

'I already do,' he answered softly, standing up and putting the last of the glass in the bin. Purposely avoiding a shocked look from Marcus, he turned to Riley who was holding an empty tin of peas. 'What do you got there?'

'It's my arachnid death chamber,' Riley answered, admiring the heavily modified tin. 'It's really easy, you just wait for the spider to crawl in and wham!'

'Take him with you!' Hester pushed Riley in front of Marcus. 'I can't stand anymore talk of those traps, they're doing my head in.'

'That's not hard,' Marcus mumbled to Benjamin.

'Besides,' Hester shot Marcus a stern look, 'I don't want to go out in the cold, and your school is just across the car park from his.'

The three jostled with shoes and jackets until they all stumbled out the door, leaving Hester who was still moaning that the school day wasn't long enough and kids should stay at school until at least six o'clock in the evening. They had just come onto the walkway when Marcus asked the question Benjamin knew was coming.

'You okay mate?'

'Fine, just broke a glass is all,' Benjamin kept his head down. He didn't like lying to Marcus, but he had decided when he got back from Meridia that it was best if his friends knew as little as possible about what he was up to during his time away. He had been shocked when they told him about Motley disappearing into grains of sand in front of them. He was convinced that Motley had something to do with Meridia, and so he figured the least the others knew, the safer they were.

'Well, anyways, here,' Marcus shoved a piece of paper that had been folded many times in to Benjamin's hand.'

'Another one?' Benjamin asked. 'This is like the fifth one this week.'

'It keeps you in practice,' Marcus responded. They kept walking along the street, Riley slightly ahead of them, singing about it being the last day of school before Christmas break.

'Marcus, the coded notes are great, but I don't need any practice. The codes you created are brilliant and I've memorized all of them. I almost got caught with one of these yesterday by Hester.'

'That's the brilliance of it, see? It's in code, so no one but us ever knows what it says. Anyways, it's the last day of term so we'll be using it loads to communicate during the break.'

'I guess,' he put the note in his pocket. 'Hey, do you think we'll get anything for Christmas this year?'

Benjamin knew the answer, but was hoping for a miracle.

'Who'd want anything from Hester, that hateful old bat,' Marcus' sneer turned into a smile. 'But you never know, seeing as it's your birthday as well, your new teacher might get you something.'

Benjamin blushed. 'What makes you think she'd do that?' He asked defensively.

'No reason.' Marcus shrugged his shoulders. 'It's just that you keep going on about how nice she is. Oh, and I think you've mentioned how pretty she is too.'

'I have not!'

'-about a hundred times,' Marcus finished and pushed Benjamin playfully.

'Hardly,' responded Benjamin.

'Hardly what? Hardly nice or hardly pretty? And all the times you've gone over to her house.'

'She's helping me with my math,' Benjamin tried to make it sound boring, but Marcus was right. Benjamin's new teacher Mrs Wink had taken an instant liking to him. Since the beginning of the school year Benjamin had been staying behind for extra help. When Mrs Wink suggested they start meeting at her house so Benjamin could meet her husband, it was like his world had brightened.

Mr Wink was a short, portly man with thick glasses that hugged the side of his round head. When he talked his short, thick tongue created a strong lisp. But Benjamin didn't care, because over the past few months he and Mr Wink had gotten quite close, both of them sharing an interest in model airplanes. Now most of Benjamin's time at the Wink's was spent visiting rather than doing maths, but he daren't tell Marcus that.

'Nah, I don't blame you,' Marcus continued. 'Everyone wants Mrs Wink as their teacher, she's well nice.'

Riley backtracked towards them. 'Benjamin, why did you break that glass?'

'What glass?'

'The glass back at the house.'

'Oh. I wasn't watching what I was doing.'

'Why?'

'Because I was looking at something else,' Benjamin said patiently.

'Did you see a spider?' Riley asked.

'No.'

'Did you see Motley?'

'No Riley, I didn't see Motley this morning.'

'Motley scares me when I see him. Especially when he comes in to our room.'

Marcus and Benjamin looked at each other. 'Riley you never told me he comes in to our room.'

Riley walked a bit further and looked around. 'He told me he'd put bugs in my bed if I told anyone,' his voice dropped to a whisper.

'When was this?' Marcus asked.

'A few days ago, a few weeks ago. It was the last time he caught me watching him.'

'What are you talking about? He's been in there before?'

'Uh-huh.'

'And you've seen him?'

Riley nodded. 'But he never saw me those times because I was in my bed behind my bug tent.'

Marcus looked at Benjamin blankly. 'Don't ask.'

'What does he do?'

'He goes through your stuff, Benjamin. Like he's looking for something.'

'Is it like last year when he was going through stuff? You remember when we thought Benjamin had run away and you woke me up that time?' Marcus had stopped walking, the others followed suit.

'Kind of, but he's whispering all the time now, saying *where is it* and he gets really angry when he can't find it. And once it sounded like he was talking to someone.'

'Who?' Benjamin and Marcus asked at the same time.

Riley shrugged. 'I didn't recognise the voice.'

'What were they saying?' Benjamin asked.

'Stuff.'

'What kind of stuff? C'mon Riley.' Marcus' impatience surprised Benjamin.

'The other person said *she's getting impatient* and *you're failing.*' Riley's bottom lip started to tremble.

'It's okay, Motley won't hurt you,' Marcus patted Riley on the back.

Benjamin started walking. 'We better get going.' He kept his head down, careful to not let the others see how hard he was thinking.

'So, Riley, were did the other person go? And how did he get there?' Marcus asked. 'Are you sure this really happened?'

'I'm not lying Marcus!' Riley rounded on him. 'It's true. They came through the window. I don't care if you don't believe me, but it's true. They don't like Motley either, because they called him furry.'

Marcus started to laugh. 'What are you on about?'

Benjamin stopped walking and grabbed Riley's shoulder. 'Was it *furry* or *fury*?'

Riley looked up at Benjamin. 'Um, it was *fury*.'

'Oh my-' Benjamin let go of Riley's shoulder.

'What? What is it? What does that mean?' Marcus had a hold of Benjamin's arm, prying him for answers.

It took Benjamin a minute to recover. 'Nothing. It's stupid, isn't it? Just creepy and scary.'

'You know something,' Marcus tried to stop Benjamin but he kept on walking through the school gates. 'What is he looking for?'

'What? I don't know. I'll run Riley to school, see you later.'

'This isn't over,' Marcus called out behind them.

Slipping in to school late didn't endear Benjamin to his teacher, Mrs Wink, who gave him a stern look when he caught up to his class going down the corridor for morning assembly. Her scolding look was lost on him, mainly because of how lovely he thought she was. With golden hair the colour of honey falling to her shoulders and eyes to match, Benjamin was totally drawn in. But today he had other things playing on his mind, and his name was Motley. Since he had been back from Meridia he had suspected Motley was involved somehow, but couldn't be sure. But now, it seemed as though he was not only involved but was more important in Meridia than even Benjamin would have guessed. The headteacher droned on in the corridor, ushering the students in to the hall. Was

Motley the man with no face in Benjamin's dreams? Why is he called Fury in Meridia? Is he even human? And what was he doing at Hadley Priest?

He needed help, and he decided he was going to tell Marcus everything after school.

'Benjamin. Benjamin are you okay?' Mrs Wink had come right up beside him before he noticed her.

'Er – I'm fine,' he jammed his hands in his pockets and kept walking.

'Are you sure?' Her concern was obvious. 'You're coming over to the house later, right?' Benjamin smiled and nodded. 'Good,' she said moving away, 'you can help us decorate the Christmas tree.'

Then someone hooked his elbow and pulled him back.

'Marcus, what are you doing?'

'Ssh,' Marcus led him around a corner. 'I told you this wasn't over. What's going on?'

'Marcus, I-'

Then a huge hand on each of their heads. 'Inside.' The headmasters' deep voice followed them as they were guided towards the hall.

Taking two seats at the back, they had only sat through a few boring minutes of assembly when things started happening. Benjamin saw a bunch of sand gather around his feet, crawling up his leg. Then the lights in the hall went out.

'Aah!' He stood up, shaking sand off his right leg. It continued up past his knee.

Then the fire door burst open, bringing a bitterly cold wind. Children and teachers stirred with surprise as some tried to close the door without success. Excitement filled the room as teachers called for calm.

'What are you doing?' Marcus hissed to Benjamin, who by this time was shaking his whole body as the sand covered him.

'Mot – Motley.' He was barely heard over the increasing volume in the hall.

'What?' Marcus said with a puzzled look.

Quickly, like hundreds of little spiders, the sand covered his face and neck.

His eyes shut tight, Benjamin gripped the Arcrux with one hand while trying to brush the sand off with the other. Sounds of disorder filled his ears, and he felt people sliding and jostling all around him.

'Marcus, help me.' Benjamin spat through clenched teeth. 'It's Motley, I know it is.' The dust formed a serpentine around his neck, pressing through Benjamin's clenched fist.

'Hang on, I'll be right back. I got an idea,' Marcus said, leaving Benjamin standing alone.

It felt like ages, standing there on his own. Children were jostling around him now, some trodding on his toes. Chairs scraped against the floor as they were hastily thrown aside. Teachers bellowed for order. The sand started to inch its way through Benjamin's tightened grip.

'Brace yourself!' He turned to Marcus' voice and was thrown off his feet by a blast of water. The torrent continued as Benjamin gasped for air. After a few minutes it reduced to a trickle and he opened his eyes to see Marcus standing above him with a dripping fire hose in his hand.

'What?' Marcus shrugged. 'It worked, didn't it?'

'Where is he? It was Motley, I know it was.'

They both searched around but could see nothing. Dripping wet, Benjamin crawled on all fours through the chairs until he bumped in to a pair of legs in a suit. He looked up in to the angry eyes of the headteacher.

Despite pleading their case, they were both sent to detention before being made to clean up the water. Exhausted, both boys trudged home to a cold dinner which included Hester barking at them to go right to bed afterwards. There was no use trying to sneak out to go to the Winks' now. Mrs Wink would probably not want to see him after today, anyways. He lay awake, fingering the Arcrux with one hand, the stone wrapped in his other. Things were getting crazy, but he was too tired to talk to Marcus tonight. He closed his eyes and went right to sleep.

He dreamed he was at the Winks' decorating their Christmas tree. Mrs Wink turned to him, laughing... His dream changed...

...behind her, the Christmas tree burst into flames. Mr Wink turned to Benjamin... his head had changed to a fierce beast. ...Benjamin looked down... black dust had come in from outside ... Mrs Wink was sent flying towards the burning Christmas tree ...

Benjamin woke with a start, his eyes fixed on the ceiling. Too disturbed to move, he lay there listening to Riley snoring, trying to push the dream out of his mind. 'She's fine,' he said repeatedly under his breath. Finally, reckless worry took over and he climbed out of bed and got dressed. Creeping past Hester's room, the clock on the wall read 10:30 when he slipped his shoes on and left the house.

Snowflakes came to rest on his hair and shoulders. His feet pushed through the powdery snow, sending it in all directions.

As he walked down the road and turned the corner towards the Winks' house, anger at missing his evening with them surfaced. All because of this stupid Arcrux. Hadn't he risked his life in Meridia without so

24

much as a thank-you? And without knowing if he would ever go back through the cellar door again, it seemed cruel that he should have to fight to keep the Arcrux safe here, too.

Coming to the front of their house, he stood outside for quite some time, watching the outlines of Mr and Mrs Wink against the curtains. The decorated Christmas tree twinkled in the window, its white fairy lights sparkling from underneath the baubles and garland.

Tears stung his eyes. He walked up to knock on the door when something caught his attention. To his right he just caught the back of someone slip around the corner of the house. His hand just over the door, ready to knock, he shot around the other side of the detached house and peered around the corner. Just as he suspected, Motley's familiar figure started to come around to the front. Without waiting he raced around the back, jumped the fence and ran full tilt back to Hadley Priest. Gasping, he burst in to the house as the cellar door was starting to rattle. The portrait of Hadley Priest was alive once again, biting its nails, looking from Benjamin to the front door.

'Go through before he comes back. Quickly now.'

Benjamin swung the cellar door open at the same time as Motley burst in the house. Without a word he flung himself down the stairs, the door slamming shut behind him.

3

Taymar Europa

Benjamin landed face down in the same clearing as he had the last time he came to Meridia. His heart leapt as he looked around to see the same seven stone markers around him. Nothing had changed, save for the snow that covered the ground and weighed down the trees.

'Yes,' he said as he rolled over on his back. 'Finally.' He stood up and brushed himself off. He found the path which, although covered in snow, was just visible through the trees. Without waiting he started down it, confident he would meet up with Jeems and Primrose.

He walked along, looking ahead for Jeems. His steps got less confident as he came across a part of the path he could not remember seeing before. The twilight was lost in the dense forest, and as time wore on he started to shiver.

Crunching snow ahead made him stop. 'Who's there?' His voice quivered. 'Jeems? Primrose?' He called out, straining to see through the darkness.

The sudden hand on his shoulder made him jump. He turned quickly and looked in to the eyes of the stranger.

'Who are you?' He asked, his breath sending a wisp of smoke in to the cold air.

An old woman stood beside him, motionless and quiet. The kerchief around her head was tied tightly under her chin, hiding a tangled mass of coarse grey hair.

'Are you – are you looking for me?' Benjamin asked through chattering teeth. The woman nodded. 'Did Gideon send you?'

The woman motioned for Benjamin to follow her and turned down the path. He ignored the uneasiness that had crept in and set off after her. She walked slowly, her feet inching along the frozen ground. She didn't make a sound except for her heavy, even breathing. A few minutes later the woman made a sharp turn to her right off the path.

'Er – wait,' Benjamin stopped a few feet behind her. 'I think you're going the wrong way. We're supposed to stay on the path.'

The woman turned and faced him. He stepped back as she moved towards him.

'I don't think we're meant to go off the path. I think I should get back to the clearing.'

Suddenly the woman shrieked and looked at her feet. Snakes and other insects poured from her trousers and sleeves.

Benjamin felt his blood turn cold. His whole body trembled as he forced himself to turn and run. Stumbling on a large root, he started to climb a tree when he heard yelling from the path ahead.

'Jeems I'm over here!' Insects and snakes covered the ground below, making their way up the tree towards him.

From above, the tree shook. Benjamin managed to get onto a large branch before another person came sliding down. Her long hair flew in front of her face as she landed firmly on the snowy ground. With lightening speed she took a long whip from her belt, snapped it with a *crack* and wrapped it tightly around the old woman's neck. She immediately collapsed in to a pile of skin, causing an avalanche of snakes, scorpions and insects to come pouring out.

The woman recoiled the whip and began to jump on top of them, trampling them with both feet.

'I will trample you and send you back in to the ground! You can do no harm here,' she called out.

She looked up at Benjamin in the tree. 'Come, young warrior. You must trample them to death.'

Benjamin shook his head. 'They'll kill me.'

'That is a lie,' she responded. 'They cannot harm you. You have been given the power to stomp them out of this world. You will not be harmed.'

Relunctantly, he closed his eyes and jumped from the tree, landing on top of the swarm. The crunching sound under his feet was matched only by the strange woman's exotic voice.

'You will not take over this place. This land is under one rule. I command you back to your depths.'

Then a more familiar voice. 'Hang on Benjermin, we're comin'.'

Benjamin looked up to see Jeems striding towards him. Primrose was behind him, timidly squashing everything in her path.

'Jeems!' he cried.

'Get outta here ya filth,' Jeems shouted at the ground and started stomping. He joined the other two and before long everything from the old woman's body had vanished in to the earth.

Fear left him as Benjamin greeted Jeems with a huge smile. Jeems came up and tousled his hair.

'It's good ter see ya, so it is.'

'You too. And you too Primrose,' Benjamin laughed as the dragon pushed her snout under his arm.

'We should not linger,' commented the strange woman from the tree.

'I see ya've met Taymar,' Jeems said.

Benjamin looked over to the woman. 'Er – '

'No, Jeems, we have not had the pleasure. I thought it best we took care of business first.'

Benjamin swallowed hard.

'Now look here, Taymar Europa, ya'll be scarin' the lad even more, so ya will.'

Taymar shook her head. 'There is no need to fear,' she said and turned to Benjamin. Benjamin let the woman approach him. With straight black hair that fell to her waist and almond-shaped eyes, she looked and spoke like she had come from some faraway place. She was dressed in a black suit that was fortified with metal buckles across her arms and legs. On her belt she had a long sword in a sheath, a dagger and the whip she had used earlier.

She held out her hand to Benjamin. 'Pleased to meet you, little warrior.' She bowed her head slightly. 'I am Taymar Europa, called here by Gideon to help you against Magh's army.'

'Er – I thought Jeems -' Benjamin stopped talking, speechless by the height of the woman standing next to him. He had never seen someone like her before; her olive skin, her sharp facial features.

'But we needs back up,' Jeems cut in. 'Since our run-in with ol' Er, Magh's bin steppin' it up a bit, so she has. Tryin' ter get every livin' thing – an' otherwise ter stop ya from comin' back.'

'I can believe it,' Benjamin muttered, thinking of Motley.

'Well,' Jeems continued, 'Gideon reckoned we could use a hand so he sent fer Taymar. Ya know, to help with the fightin' and the like.'

'And I see I've come not a moment too soon,' Taymar added and looked over to where the old woman had stood.

'Was that Magh?' Benjamin asked after a moment of silence.

Taymar shook her head. 'No, little warrior, but it is Magh who sent her and it is at least Magh, if not something worse that took her soul.'

'There's worse?' Benjamin looked from Taymar to Jeems. 'I thought Magh was the worst anybody could get. And where did the woman come from? I thought we were the only people left in Meridia.'

Jeems and Taymar looked at each other. 'Like I said, there's bin lots goin' on since ya were here last. That there lady is not the first one to -'

'- to fall in the hands of a liar,' Taymar cut in. 'The rest, little warrior, will have to wait for Gideon. He is your teacher and the one who will answer your questions.'

Taymar turned and led them out of the trees and back onto the path. When Jeems stopped to help Primrose get a thorn out of her foot, Benjamin hung back as well.

'Jeems,' he whispered as he looked over his shoulder. 'Who is she?'

'Who? Oh, Taymar.' Jeems looked up briefly. 'She's known Gideon fer ages, so she has. Reckons she fought with Gideon in the last battle Meridia seen, but that was ages and ages ago.'

'So what is she doing here?'

Jeems patted Primrose. 'There ya go darlin'. All better. Aw, don't go actin' all injured now.' He started walking with Benjamin.

'Like she said, Gideon sent fer her. After things started gettin' outta hand. I guess he figures she'll come in handy.'

The hairs on the back of his neck prickled. 'What's been going on?'

'It's too risky ter talk here. Gideon'll tell ya everything.' Benjamin's face dropped. 'Sorry mate,' Jeems continued. 'Gideon made us promise that we'd just come an' get ya an' leave the rest ter him.'

Annoyed, Benjamin didn't respond. He looked ahead to Taymar. Her strides were swift and sure and Benjamin thought he could hear something.

'Is she singing?'

Jeems cocked his head and nodded. 'Sounds like it. But don't be serprised if ya can't understand her. She speaks more languages then ya'd think possible. And a few that don't even exist in this world.'

Benjamin slowed his pace and watched her intently. 'She's kinda -'

'- in yer face?' Jeems smiled and nodded. 'Don't let that get ter ya. She's one of the good ones, she is. But I see what yer sayin'. I found her a bit strange at first meself.'

The group walked along in silence. Jeems would occasionally tell Benjamin what Primrose had been up to, and Benjamin, when asked, would tell Jeems about Riley and Marcus. After walking for what seemed like ages, the familiar sound of leaves rustling caused them all to stop. Just like the last time Benjamin had come to Meridia, the path ahead of them had become blocked, swallowed up with swollen trees and angry looking vines.

'Ugh. Finally.' Benjamin stumbled backwards. 'We can stop.' He crumpled down on the path, laying flat on his back.

'Do not get too comfortable, little warrior,' Taymar said as she studied the thorns. 'It is not safe. You must always be on your guard.'

Taymar took a step back and spoke loudly in to the dark air. 'You have no right to keep us prisoner, Magh. This simple trick of your dark magic is not enough to hold us.' Taymar looked around at the trees for a moment, as if waiting for a response.

34

Everything was quiet, except for Primrose's chattering teeth. Suddenly Benjamin felt the wind pick up. The coldness stung his cheeks and blew through their hair. Then the voices came. All three looked up as a murmuring of voices picked up from the blackened trees.

Jeems gripped his pack tightly and scolded Primrose when she trampled on his feet because her eyes were covered.

Benjamin strained to understand what the voices were saying. 'You will not understand them, little warrior,' Taymar insisted. 'It is a dark language and they are full of lies, so what they are saying is not important.' They stood back to back, looking towards the trees as the voices got louder. They seemed to wrap themselves around the four, swirling between them, whispering hateful chants in Benjamin's ears.

'You are not welcome here!' Taymar called out. She took a breath and started speaking in a language Benjamin had never heard. She raised her hands towards the trees and they shrank and changed colour. The voices, louder at first, started to trail off. Taymar turned to the path and pushed her hand through the tangled mass of thorns and prickly leaves. They recoiled instantly and, with a final lingering whisper, the path was clear.

Benjamin wasn't sure if he was shaking from the cold or from what he had just seen. 'Oh my -'

'-Gideon.' Jeems finished. Benjamin looked up to see the familiar old man standing ahead of them along the side of the path.

'I am so glad to see you all in one piece,' Gideon said, his eyes scanning the group until they rested on Primrose. 'It's over now, Primrose. You can open your eyes.'

Embarrassed, the little dragon peeked through her thick fingers and a blinding light pierced the dark.

Gideon turned to Taymar. 'I think we will take the short way home.' Taymar bowed her head while Gideon turned towards Jeems and Benjamin. 'Anybody for a cup of tea?' He asked as he walked off the path and through the trees. Taymar followed him and then Primrose, who was more than happy to be leaving the forest. Benjamin looked at Jeems.

'It's awright,' Jeems reassured Benjamin. 'Just follow Primrose and ya'll come out with the rest of them. I'll be right behind ya.'

After a few cautious steps through the trees, Benjamin found himself next to the others in front of the waterfall that led to Water's Hyde.

They waited for a few minutes. 'Where's Jeems?' Benjamin finally asked.

Gideon and Taymar exchanged a concerned look. 'We'll wait a few moments,' Gideon finally responded. Benjamin watched Primrose rock up and down on her hind legs nervously, trying not to fix his eyes on the spot where Jeems should have come out.

Finally Gideon broke the tension. 'Benjamin and Primrose, you will both come with me through to Water's Hyde.' He turned to Taymar, who gave an understanding nod. 'Make haste,' he said to her in a low voice. She turned and ran towards the edge of the forest.

Gideon stretched out his arms. 'Come along you two, let's go get that cup of tea.'

4

Missing

Water's Hyde was just as Benjamin remembered it. Everything was still in its place, except for Jeems who by now was officially missing.

'I need not remind you to make yourself at home?' Gideon shuffled towards the table.

Methodically Benjamin took a seat at the table on one of the benches. He noticed Primrose sniffing the couch Jeems usually slept on before she curled up in front of it.

Gideon looked up from where he stood by the fire. 'There, there Primrose,' he said tenderly. 'Jeems will be with us soon. Taymar will find him.'

'What happened to him?'

'It could simply be that Jeems missed the aperture I had created, possibly leaving him behind. It does not stay open for long. Gideon studied the portrait over the fire. 'But I think that is a most unlikely explanation.'

Primrose stared straight ahead, her vacant eyes full of sorrow.

'I strongly suspect that he has been captured by Magh, or more specifically, by whoever she sent to do it for her.'

'Magh?' Benjamin straightened up. 'What would Magh want with Jeems?' He slumped on his seat. 'I bet they were after me.'

Gideon handed Benjamin a drink and sat down across from him. 'I'm not so sure you were the focus of their attention at that moment.' Benjamin shook his head slightly, unable to understand. 'The fact that you managed to secure the Earth League previously and make it back to Meridia has certainly caused Magh to become more active.' Their eyes met. 'But I don't think a mistake was made in who they took prisoner tonight. I am convinced they meant to capture Jeems.'

Benjamin furled his eyebrows. 'Why?'

'The answer to your question would be best told by Jeems. But, I will say that Magh's primary reason would be to try and delay the next part of your journey.'

'So what can we do?'

'We can keep positive and busy ourselves here while Taymar finds Jeems and brings him back.'

'What if she never finds him?'

Gideon smiled. 'Taymar is an expert tracker and I'm sure she will have found help along the way. That, and, based on what you saw of her in the forest earlier, I'm sure you would agree that Taymar can take care of herself.

Feeling slightly reassured, Benjamin turned to Primrose. 'She doesn't look so good.'

Gideon sighed. 'I'm afraid she will most likely remain that way until Jeems is back with us safe and sound.'

'She sure misses him.'

'Very much so,' Gideon nodded. 'They have been together for quite some time now. The story of how they found each other is fascinating.'

'How did it happen?' Benjamin asked, happy to be distracted.

'You should ask Jeems to tell it to you when he comes back,' Gideon replied with a wink.

'Do you really think he's going to be okay?'

Gideon nodded.

'How can you be so sure?'

'I'm sure.'

There was nothing left to do. As much as Benjamin wanted to ask Gideon what had been going on in Meridia, his thoughts were fixed on Jeems.

'I suspect you are tired and your thoughts are with Jeems. May I suggest we turn in for the night? You will find your room as you left it.'

Without another word Benjamin got up and headed down the corridor. Entering the room he found it the same as he left it, with a fresh hot drink and chocolate biscuits on the side table. He crawled in to bed, his stomach churning.

He tossed and turned for what seemed like ages, trying to block out the horrible thoughts of what Magh was doing to Jeems. He moved in and out of a restless sleep until his body relaxed and he fell in to a dream.

Benjamin dreamed he was floating along the ceiling of Hadley Priest, looking down on Hester, Riley and Marcus.

'Where in the name of Christopher did he get to this time?' Hester cried. She paced across the floor. 'There's going to be questions, maybe even an inquiry. They'll be wondering what kind of place I'm running.'

'What kind of place you're sinking, you mean,' muttered Marcus.

'You'd do best to keep your gums closed,' Hester retorted. 'They'll shut this place down and you'll be on the streets.'

'No.' Riley protested. He looked at Marcus who shook his head reassuringly.

'No one knows we even exist,' Marcus mouthed the words. Riley began to sob.

'Now look what you've done, you bone idle fool,' Hester said angrily. 'He'll be at it for the rest of the night, and I'll -'

Hester stopped in mid-sentence as she looked past Marcus. Following her gaze Marcus turned and saw Motley.

'Having a family meeting?' His voice barely audible.

'Not likely,' said Marcus. He turned to Hester, but only her back as she left the house, closing the front door behind her. 'Waster,' he said, watching her head towards the pub through the window.

Motley turned to Riley who was still crying. 'I don't like kids. Especially when they cry.' Riley had a look of fear painted on his face.

'Leave him alone, Motley,' Marcus said. 'He's just a little upset, is all.'

'Oh,' Motley said in a mocking tone and cocked his head. He looked down at Riley. 'Missing your little friend, are you?'

'Shut up!' Marcus snapped. 'As if you don't know where he is.' Then, remembering himself, stepped back slightly.

Motley's eyes narrowed as he looked at Marcus. 'What exactly are you trying to say?' he hissed.

Riley stood beside Marcus. 'We saw you -'

'Shut up Riley,' Marcus nudged his elbow and gave him a scolding look.

'I don't want you to see anything that might scare you, so I'll make sure it doesn't happen again.' In one motion Motley whipped Riley's glasses off and flung them to the floor. Then he gripped Riley by the neck and lifted him off his feet.

'Get off him,' Marcus cried and went for Motley but was pushed back against the wall. He just got up when the entire house shook violently, all three struggling to keep their balance. A crack like a gunshot sent vibrations along the walls and a loud, booming voice came out of nowhere. 'Leave him.' The voice echoed through the house.

Motley's hand began to smoke and turn black. Bewildered, he dropped Riley and left. Marcus ran to Riley, collapsed on the floor. 'You're okay,' Marcus said over and over....

.....his dream changed ...

Benjamin was walking along a forest path. He heard something ahead and began to run towards it. He stumbled in to a clearing. In the clearing were seven stone markers. He looked up and saw Jeems hanging in mid-air, blood running down his face. Benjamin stepped back and bumped in to a toad-like creature with mangled hair. Benjamin backed away from it and fell down.

He woke up on the floor of his room at Water's Hyde, shaking and looking around. He found his voice. 'Jeems.'

He stumbled out of his blankets and down the corridor towards the main room, the torches burning bright as he walked past. He looked around. The fire had died down to glowing embers and he couldn't see Gideon. He went over to where Primrose was sleeping.

'Primrose wake up. Primrose,' Benjamin whispered, nudging her snout. 'Wake up. I know where Jeems is.'

5

Lost and Found

Streaks of light burst from the little dragon's eyes. Her head shot up to attention.

'I know where Jeems is, I think. I had a dream about him,' Benjamin recovered, squinting from the bright light.

Primrose cocked her head to one side and looked at Benjamin.

'Listen, Primrose. I get these dreams that – that come true sometimes but not every time. Anyways, I had a dream about where Jeems is. He's in trouble Primrose, we've got to help him.'

Primrose snorted softly and a single wisp of smoke rose out of her right nostril. She motioned to a portrait of Gideon on the wall behind her, a worried look on her face.

'I know Gideon didn't want us to go with Taymar to find Jeems so I don't think he'd be too wild about us going out now. But Gideon isn't here and Jeems is in a lot of danger. We need to get to him.'

Primrose nodded nervously, and stretched her legs before standing to her full height. Benjamin got dressed and grabbed his pack and his staff, jogging back to where the little dragon was waiting.

'Okay Primrose, hopefully we'll be able to get through the waterfall without Gideon.' Primrose snorted louder and shook her head.

'Well, it's the only way out.'

Primrose pointed her snout towards the ceiling. Benjamin looked up. 'Primrose what are you on about, there is no ceiling,' then it dawned on him. 'Is that how you get in and out? Through the top of the mountain.'

Primrose nodded.

'That's great, but, how am I going to get up there? You're too sharp to ride,' he said, rubbing the scars on his stomach.

Primrose fanned out her wings and bent her legs. With one huge push she lifted off the ground, Benjamin's hair rustling with the force. She grabbed the collar of his shirt with her hind legs and lifted him up in to the mountain.

'Whoa,' his stomach flipped. Primrose's eyes shone like two lanterns through the darkness. Her little wings flapped fast and furious with the extra weight.

'Come on Primrose, it can't be much further,' he called out to her.

A few moments later and they had come to rest on a wide ledge. Taking some time to catch her breath, Primrose sniffed around on the wall until she found the spot she was looking for. She scratched her claws three times on the spot, and a blanket of dead ivy that was stuck to the mountain wall dropped. A crooked doorway had been cut in to the wall, the stone resting loosely inside the opening.

'Primrose, you've got your own secret entrance!'

Primrose bawled and pushed the stone away from the door. Except for the stars that dotted the sky, the darkness was as thick outside as it was inside the mountain top. The cold air hit Benjamin's face and he immediately started to shiver.

'We're almost at the very t-top of the m-mountain,' he looked turned to Primrose. 'You wouldn't be able to fly both of us to Jeems, would you?' Primrose shook her head and fanned out her little wings. 'No, I suppose you're too little to carry me that far.'

Primrose moaned slightly and bowed her head.

'It's okay. It's not a bad thing,' Benjamin responded quickly. 'If you were any bigger you'd scare the life out of me,' he thought for a moment. 'But could you give me a lift down?'

Primrose pushed off and grabbed Benjamin again, gliding them down towards the ground.

As soon as they landed, Primrose's nerves started to get the better of her. Her movements were short and jerky, with her head spinning from side to side.

'It's okay, Primrose. We just need to stay focused. No one is watching us,' Benjamin swallowed hard. 'Okay. In my dream I saw seven stone markers. It looked like the place where you and Jeems were coming to meet me. Do you know where I mean?'

Primrose nodded.

'Do you know the way from here?'

Primrose's eyes lit up and she nodded again enthusiastically. Before Benjamin could say anything else Primrose was bounding towards the edge of the forest on all fours.

'Wait up!' Benjamin ran after her.

Once in the forest, Primrose jumped at every sound, her brief excitement turning to fear.

'Primrose, calm down.' Benjamin tried to sooth her after the simultaneous hooting of an owl and scurrying of something on the ground sent her behind a tree. 'It's only an owl, and probably a wurvil,' he urged. 'Come on, Jeems needs us.' Slowly, Primrose edged out from behind the tree and they carried on.

'Is it much further?' Benjamin asked after they had walked a good few hours. 'We've been walking for ages.'

Primrose shook her head. The scurrying along side of them had gotten heavier, and was joined by a swishing noise overhead.

'There's lots of birds around,' Benjamin commented, looking up in to the trees.

Trees to the left rustled and a big black raven clipped Benjamin's right shoulder with its wing. It nosedived in to something scurrying alongside the path.

Benjamin swung around fast before checking on Primrose.

'Primrose?' The little dragon had her eyes covered, running around in circles ahead of him.

He went towards her. 'Let's get going.'

Then a voice from the trees. 'Duck!' Benjamin turned in the direction of the voice and was again grazed by the raven.

'Who's there?' Benjamin asked nervously.

A figure came towards them through the dark. The voice reached them first. 'The only one who is supposed to be here,' said Taymar, walking onto the path behind Primrose.

Benjamin let out a relieved sigh. Then more fluttering in the trees. 'Taymar, there's a raven after us. It works for Magh. I've seen it before. We've got to kill it.'

Benjamin's jaw dropped when the raven came to rest gently on Taymar's shoulder.

Fear and suspicion crept in. 'Who are you?' he demanded, bringing his staff up in front of him, gripping it tightly in both hands.

'Relax, little warrior. Your battle is not with me,' Taymar chortled. 'This,' she continued as she stroked the raven, 'has been my guide. He found me only a while ago.'

Benjamin loosened his grip. 'O-kaay. So the raven just – came out of nowhere?'

Taymar nodded. 'I am sure Gideon sent him to show me the way to Jeems. Magh's not the only one with spies.' Her eyes moved between Benjamin and Primrose. 'But it looks like I didn't need a guide but for you two. All the same, you should not have come. You have left the Arcrux vulnerable.'

'We want to help save Jeems. We know where we're going. Or at least Primrose does.' Benjamin watched the raven, still perched on Taymar's shoulder.

Taymar paused thoughtfully for a moment then shook her head. 'You will have to come with me, it will take too much time for me to return you to Water's Hyde. Hang on to your courage, little warrior, you are going to need it.'

Taking flight, the raven led the group towards the clearing, stopping just short when voices were heard up ahead. It perched on a branch a few feet above Taymar.

'I owe you many thanks,' Taymar said to the raven. 'Now go before you are missed.' The raven cocked its head and disappeared into the night.

They crept towards the voices. Drawing nearer, the orange glow from a fire flickered through the trees. An acrid smell filled the air. The clearing was in sight. Taymar stopped.

'We are very close,' she whispered. 'We will go left to find cover.' Just then a painful cry filled the air. Jeems' voice was filled with anguish. Taymar held onto Primrose's snout before she could make a sound. 'You must stay silent or we will all be caught.' Primrose snorted and Taymar slowly let her go.

The three left the path and crept along silently through thick brush until they found cover enough for all of them within sight of the clearing a safe distance away. Benjamin and Taymar had just got behind two huge trees, and Primrose behind a large boulder in front of them when another wail from Jeems sent chills up Benjamin's spine.

They turned towards the clearing, the distance making everything look slightly smaller than it actually was. The first row of trees around the clearing was laden with ravens, branches bending underneath their combined weight. A small gathering of grisly beasts huddled near the massive fire, smoke billowing from its top. On the other side Jeems was on his side, curled in a ball on the ground. His body twitched randomly, as if he was in a tormented sleep. His wrists and ankles were such that they looked as though they were tied together, but no ropes were seen. Possibly the bindings around them were invisible. Every so often Jeems would call out and try to wriggle free from them. Slashes marked his bare back, evidence that he had been hit with a whip.

Benjamin turned to Taymar. Deep creases were etched in her forehead, her eyes darting across the scene. Primrose held her head in her hands, silver tears dripping from her eyes onto the snow below.

Jeems groaned loudly and lifted his head, showing his badly beaten face. Burned and bruised, his eyes were swollen and damaged with dark purple rings around them. He tried force them open, but it was no use, his eyelids had collapsed.

'I can't see,' Jeems croaked. The only reply came from the beasts nearest him, who snarled and gnashed their teeth. One of them came close, but recoiled when Jeems started to jerk his head around. 'Who are ya and wot d'yer want?'

'Taymar! We've got to do something,' Benjamin pleaded in a high-pitched whisper. Taymar looked at him, nodded and put her finger to her lips.

'I can't see,' Jeems called out again. 'Why can't I-'

'-see?' A woman's voice cut in from behind one of the markers. She stepped out in to the firelight, her long black hair tied up in a pile on top of her head.

'Magh?' Benjamin mouthed the words to Taymar who nodded. He turned back, his heart beating faster.

Magh spoke again. 'We can't have you leading the boy to the next league now, can we Jeems. And what better way than to make sure you can't see where you're going.' As she approached Jeems, Benjamin fought back the urge to charge her. 'My dear servant Rags,' she motioned to one of the beasts, 'you remember Rags? He slobbers so much that I thought I would put it to good use, so I made him toxic,' she giggled. 'I trust it only stung for a short while. I told him not to spit on you too heavily, but you remember how clumsy he is, don't you? So I had to watch him. One bad shot and you'd have no face left. Then you'd be no use to me.'

'I'm no use ter ya, Magh. Face or not.' Jeems scrambled to a sitting position, his ankles and wrists pinned together in front of him.

Magh pursed her lips. 'No use to me? Are you sure about that?' She walked in and out of the stone markers. 'I wish you could see yourself, wriggling on the ground like a worm! You are bound solely by your own betrayal. Unable to move and you haven't even done anything for me yet!'

'Yer wastin' yer time. I'd never help the likes of ya.'

Magh stood above him, her arms crossed in front of her. 'There was a time, not long ago, when you wouldn't even think of saying such a thing.'

'I've changed,' Jeems grunted.

'Changed? Or been bought.' Magh circled him. 'Tell me, where did Gideon find you?'

'Well, ya'd know the answer ter that, wouldn't ya? T'was the place where ya left me fer dead, so it was. And it ain't none of yer business how I got in with Gideon.'

'There's no need to get defensive,' Magh stated airily. 'And I do think you're overreacting. I would say your unfortunate departure from my service was a simple misunderstanding.'

'Taymar.' Fighting back tears, Benjamin strained to see Taymar through the dark. 'Ta-'

'Shh, little warrior,' Taymar had come up behind him, her hand now over his mouth. 'I know you are troubled by what you hear, but you need to remember this; Jeems serves Gideon now. His past deeds are of no consequence to us.'

Benjamin spun around to argue but was silenced once again.

'Magh left him for dead before and she will do it again. Wait here while I go to the other side of the clearing. I will try to draw their attention to me.' Benjamin could hear the beasts snarling and fighting in the background. 'When no one is looking, you and Primrose will have to get him and drag him to safety.'

Without waiting for an answer Taymar disappeared through the trees. Benjamin turned back to Jeems, who was now hollering out. The beasts were circling him now, hitting out and snapping their teeth.

'Misunderstandin'?' Jeems croaked. 'Is that what ya call leavin' summon ter burn ter death? I'm done doin' yer dirty work. I wanted out then and I'm not about ter change me mind.'

Magh scattered the beasts with one wave of her arm. 'Yes, having you burn in lava was clever, but I can't take all the credit. Howl, our great Master came up with that idea.' She walked up to him again. 'But you see, that is where the misunderstanding comes in.' Her eyes flashed and her voice got deeper. 'You can never leave my service once you enter in to it.'

Magh swung her arm in the air and Jeems was flung upwards, hovering at least ten feet above the ground.

As if by invitation, ravens swopped down from the trees towards Jeems. They flew by him, pulling out bits of his hair as they went past. Jeems hollered in pain. The noise got so loud Benjamin chanced moving next to Primrose, who immediately hid her head underneath his arm.

'Call 'em off!' Jeems cried, throwing his head from side to side to avoid the ravens' sharp beaks.

'I'm not going to do that,' answered Magh calmly. 'As you are in my service, there is something I need you to do for me. They are there to make sure you don't need much persuading.'

'Ferget it Magh. No chance. And Howl's not Master ter anything. Not mine, anyhow.' Magh's mouth twitched. She flicked her hand towards Jeems and he started shaking violently.

'Why Jeems, you haven't even heard what it is yet,' she said casually. She drew back her hand, turning Jeems' body limp as he dropped to the ground. A trickle of blood ran down his face as he turned slowly on to his back.

'Wot is it?' Jeems managed to find his voice.

'Oh, nothing too difficult – seeing as it's your first assignment in a while.' She turned her back to him. 'I want you to stop the boy from continuing his ridiculous journey.'

'How d'yer 'xpect me ter do that?'

'You don't expect me to believe that you don't remember how we do things around here?' Magh kicked one of the beasts out of her way, making it squeal and hobble around the fire to the amusement of the others.

'Like kill him, d'ya mean?'

Benjamin and Primrose looked at each other in disbelief. Benjamin felt prickles travel up from the base of his neck.

Magh laughed. 'Well, if you insist. I mean, you're no stranger to-'

'No way Magh. I'm not doin' it.'

Magh faced Jeems again. 'Now Jeems this just isn't like you. You've never been one to turn down something so exciting.'

'You don't know me anymore.' Jeems said and hung his head.

'Oh, but I do,' Magh smiled wryly. 'There is little about you I don't know, including how you would answer me tonight. That is why I didn't even bother to bind you. You have betrayed your true Master, and that has already taken hold of you, restraining you.' She shook her head slowly. 'No matter how many times you tell yourself you have, you haven't changed a bit. You are still the same low lying, deceitful, traitorous cretin that you always were.

'No! I don't believe it. I've changed. I love that boy.' The ferocity of Jeem's scream scattered the ravens back to the trees. He struggled until his bindings snapped and he fell next to the fire. Startled for a moment, the beasts ran towards him. As they surrounded him, Benjamin saw Taymar jump over one of the stones markers.

'Leave him!' Her voice echoed through the night. The creatures turned to her, gnashing their teeth.

'You're not the only one who can do tricks,' she said to Magh. She snapped her hand towards the beasts and they were all struck blind, their mouths clamped shut.

'Stupid Sentaph!' Magh cried. 'Do you honestly think you will get out of here alive?'

Taymar looked at Magh. 'You are nothing. You haven't the authority to kill me. I was sent by another, and it is for him that I fight.' Without flinching she drew a sword that looked like it had no blade but sliced through the creature that had snuck up behind her.

From the safety of the rock, Benjamin and Primrose watched Taymar slay everything that was coming at her. As her sword struck, a brilliant light shone through the creatures where they lay. Gruesome looking creatures came out from the trees, pouncing on her from behind, but nothing penetrated her, the armour she had on as mysterious as the blade in her hand.

Benjamin moved out from behind the rock but Primrose held him back.

'What are you doing?' he asked angrily.

Primrose pointed to the Arcrux.

'I suppose you're right. It would be too close to Magh.' He looked back over and saw Jeems had crawled to the edge of the clearing and was now lying motionless on the ground, away from the battle.

'But Primrose, Taymar told me to get Jeems. This may be our only chance.' He tucked the Arcrux in his shirt. 'Stay close.' He led the way, crawling on all fours raising his head every so often to see if they had been noticed.

'Jeems?' Benjamin called out when they had got close to him. His voice almost lost in the chaos around him.

Jeems lashed out.

'It's me,' Benjamin said, shielding himself. 'Benjamin and Primrose. We're going to get you out of here.'

Jeems relaxed and started crying. Benjamin took off his cloak and wrapped it around Jeems as he hoisted him onto Primrose.

'Primrose stop moving,' but she had already jumped at the sqwaking raven directly above them, sending Jeems tumbling to the ground.

It was enough to distract a few stragglers, including Magh who by this time was on the far side of the clearing. Gliding through the air, she sped towards them, her eyes burning in to Benjamin's. A deep chill went through him, and he found himself unable to move.

Magh hovered inches above the ground in front of them, her eyes jet black. Benjamin put his arm up to shield them when Taymar came flying over top of them, a blinding light in front of her that sent Magh flying backwards.

Recovering, Magh swung her right arm at the fire and a stream of flames charged towards them. Taymar struck out her left arm and the flames turned in to water that splashed over them.

'Move aside,' Magh hissed menacingly. Despite the tone in her voice, she approached Taymar with caution.

'Do not speak to me,' Taymar demanded. 'You will allow us safe passage out of here.'

Magh hovered a few inches above the ground and then came to stand in front of Taymar.

'I'm afraid it's not that easy,' she answered. 'You will not get out of here alive.'

'You believe so many lies,' Taymar snapped. 'We will get out of here alive. Your foolish tricks are no match for the weapons I have been given.'

Suddenly a ring of blue flames shot up around the four of them. Benjamin started to run out but Taymar grabbed his arm.

'It's consuming fire,' she said to him. 'We will be with Gideon soon.'

On the other side of the flames Benjamin could hear Magh screaming in frustration. He turned again and faced the beast he had seen in his dream. Through the fire, staring back at him, their eyes met. Something in its eyes was different, as if it was pleading to be rescued. He held the beasts' gaze until they were consumed by the flames.

As the fire died down, Benjamin found himself back in the main room at Water's Hyde. Gideon strode over and effortlessly picked Jeems up and carried him to his small bed.

'What bottles do you want?' Benjamin asked, heading towards the cabinet.

'They won't be necessary, thank you Benjamin,' Gideon replied flatly, not looking up.

'Jeems,' Gideon spoke softly after he laid him down. 'You must tell me what haunts you.' He stroked Jeems' forehead and scanned the length of his broken body. 'Your body can only be healed after your spirit is.'

Jeems turned his head towards Gideon and licked his dry lips. 'Deceitful .... traitorous,' he mumbled. Tears streamed out of his mangled eyes as he spoke.

Benjamin stood alone off to the side while Taymar consoled Primrose. They all looked on in silence. Gideon took hold of Jeems' hand.

'Do you believe you have been set free from your service to Magh? And that you do not consider Howl to be your Master?' He asked. Benjamin took in breath sharply but no one seemed to notice.

After a moment, Jeems nodded.

'You have been set free because I bought you for a price. Do you believe that?'

Jeems nodded again.

'Then reject the lies told to you today. You have been set free and that is how you will remain.'

As Gideon spoke, he touched Jeems' legs and eyes. 'Open your eyes and sit up.'

Jeems did what Gideon said and within moments his eyes and body were back to normal. Primrose bounded up to Jeems and jammed her snout in his face, licking his ear.

'Get outta here, ya big baby,' Jeems laughed. 'I'll be awright. Just a few bruises left.'

The tension slowly left the room as Jeems stood up and walked over to Taymar. 'I owe ya one,' he said to her gruffly.

'You owe me nothing. I was only a distraction. It is Benjamin that pulled you out of danger.'

All eyes turned to Benjamin who felt oddly alone where he was standing. He fixed his gaze somewhere across the room as Jeems approached him.

'Benjermin-' Jeems began, searching his face.

Benjamin looked past him. 'All those things Magh said.'

Tears came back. 'I'm sorry ya had ter hear that,' Jeems explained. 'I don't – I don't know where ter start.' He sniffled and wiped his eyes. 'Ya've got ter know that I've changed, I'm not that person anymore.'

Gideon stepped up between the two. 'I think we have taken care of that once and for all,' he hugged Jeems' shoulder and ushered him over to where Taymar was standing.

'You and Taymar will go out when you feel ready,' Gideon said to Jeems.

'I want ter go now,' Jeems straightened out. Gideon was quiet.

'Magh will not expect Jeems to be travelling so soon,' Taymar suggested. 'We may take some ground.'

'Very well,' Gideon said thoughtfully.

Exhausted, Benjamin went to follow Jeems but Gideon stopped him.

'You will be staying here with me,' Gideon said in a deeper voice than Benjamin was used to.

'But what about the leagues?' Benjamin asked, watching the three go through the middle archway at the back of Water's Hyde.

'They are doing something else right now. They won't be long.' Gideon turned Benjamin to face

63

him.   'It will give you and I time to talk about what happened tonight.'

6

Prysteen

After mumbling goodbye, Benjamin sank in to the armchair by the fire, his eyes fixed on Greyfriars who was chasing a dust bunny under the table.

'I had hoped to find you in your bed last night,' Gideon began. His voice was sombre, almost full of regret.

'I wanted to help,' Benjamin muttered, shrugging his left shoulder. Greyfriars jumped on and then off his lap, leaving him to play with his fingers.

'Hmm.' Gideon raised his eyebrows. 'And from what I understand you were very helpful. But at what cost? Are you comfortable with everything you saw and heard last night?'

There was a long silence while Benjamin thought about his answer. 'I don't know. No, I guess not. I didn't understand most of it.' His feet swung gently, and he glanced over to Gideon who was looking at the portrait over the hearth.

'I'm not surprised to hear you say that, and it is one of the reasons why I didn't ask you to go with Taymar that night. The primary reason, of course, was your safety. However, the safety of the Arcrux needs to be taken seriously.' Gideon turned to Benjamin. 'You have been trusted with Meridia's future.' His tone softened and he sighed deeply. 'Alas, we now have a situation where you know things that for the most part do not make any sense to you, am I right?'

Benjamin nodded.

'I trust you have questions?'

Benjamin shifted in his chair. 'Well, yeah. But about loads of stuff, not just last night. Before Meridia nothing happened to me, my life was really boring. And now, everything has just exploded. Stuff isn't just going on here but at Hadley Priest also. One of my housemates Motley, turned to sand right in front of me. I know he's trying to get the Arcrux from me. And Taymar is a bit strange. She talks in strange languages and has some weird magic sword, and she's always on about how great you are – not that that's a bad thing,' Benjamin added quickly. 'The stuff about Jeems has freaked me out, but I was freaked out way before that. None of it makes sense. The first time I left Meridia I thought I knew what was going on, but now I'm just as confused as I was before.'

Benjamin looked around before continuing. 'The reason why I woke up last night was because I had a dream about where Jeems was. More and more of my dreams are like that, showing me things. Sometimes my dreams actually happen.' Gideon turned to him and their eyes met. 'What's happening to me?'

'The first thing you must know, Benjamin, is that it is not my intention for you to come to any harm either here or back at Hadley Priest. Neither is it the intention of Jeems or Taymar, or anyone else that I may introduce you to. Our common interest is seeing you safely through your journey. I can understand why you have been so troubled. I only hope you can understand that I will not be able to make everything clear to you. And as I have told you before, some of it will only be made clear to you through experience. Your dreams are clearly messages, and you will begin to learn how you can use them to your advantage.' Gideon sat down in the other armchair. 'Nothing Taymar uses is magic, you must know that. Magic is used by the likes of Magh and her minions. The weapons Taymar uses are definitely not of the world you are familiar with, but they are based in goodness and truth nonetheless. And I'm glad she speaks highly of me. She should. Meridia was my idea.'

Gideon held up his hand to silence Benjamin who could only utter sounds of amazement. 'Please, it sounds much more glamorous than it is, and I don't like to boast. My story is best kept for another time, as there are more pressing matters to deal with. But Taymar is a servant of mine, she is one of many Sentaphs. She is not a human, although she looks like it to you now. She is from the parallel world that has gone on since almost the beginning of time, and it is this world that you are now able to see, Benjamin. That is why you could see Motley turn in to dust. You have been given eyes to see both worlds.

Benjamin was quiet for a moment. 'So Motley is from here too?'

Gideon nodded.

'So is Motley a Sentaph?'

'That is a very interesting question,' Gideon explained. 'Sentaphs are a specific kind of being. Motley is what is known as a Raptor. They are the opposite of Sentaphs.'

'So what's the difference between the two?'

'Simply put, Sentaphs are on our side and Raptors are not. The main similarity is that they are not normally seen by humans.'

Benjamin sighed. 'Right.'

'Since Meridia was created, Raptors have wanted nothing more than to rule it,' Gideon explained. 'They thought they could do that by getting humans on their side. The more people they were able to lure in to doing horrible things, the stronger the Raptors got. So the Sentaphs have been very busy trying to keep the Raptors as far away as possible.'

'So that's why there are bad people in the world?'

Gideon nodded.

'And Magh?'

Gideon stroked his beard. 'Magh was created by Howl, the leader of the Raptors.'

'So Magh works for this *Howl* – where did he come from?' Benjamin could almost hear his mind whirring.

'Now that is a marvellous story, but I am convinced that what we are talking about now is quite enough to deal with.'

Benjamin moaned disapprovingly.

Gideon smiled and shook his head. 'But for now,' he stood up and went over to where the portrait hung over the hearth, 'I think you deserve to know how Magh was created.'

Gideon went over to the hearth and lifted the massive portrait down from the wall. As he laid it flat on the floor, the portrait changed from a landscape to smoking swirls on a black canvas. Standing over it, he held out his hand to Benjamin.

Hesitating slightly, Benjamin got up and stood beside Gideon. They both looked down at the portrait for a few moments before Benjamin finally asked, 'what are we doing?'

'Hm?' Gideon raised his eyebrows. 'Oh. We're waiting for the right time. You may or may not have noticed this portrait when you first came to Water's Hyde.'

69

Benjamin nodded. 'It moves.'

'That it does. Through the ages of time.'

'But it's all black, with some smoke. How do you know when the right time is?'

'I know.' A few moments passed. 'We're just waiting for the right time to – Ah, here we are. So if you will take my hand.'

Following along, Benjamin stood on the moving portrait with smoky wisps rising from the canvas. Suddenly, the portrait gave way and he found himself freefalling with Gideon into darkness.

The smoky wisps caught them and they started floating gently down. His body relaxed as he drifted along until Gideon pulled his hand to the right and they settled softly on the grass of a sleepy town.

People walked by Benjamin, not noticing him.

'Gideon, where are we? And who are all these people?'

'I'm not surprised you don't recognise it,' Gideon responded. 'It looked much different when you were here last.'

Benjamin looked around blankly. 'Was I born here?'

'No, but this is where it all began, in a manner of speaking. We are in the town of Prysteen, one of the many that existed in Meridia.'

Benjamin turned just in time to side step two people galloping on horseback.

'There is no need,' Gideon said. 'They cannot see us. What you are seeing now is in the past; one of my many memories.'

Lush grass and gardens blanketed the area. To the one side was a large clump of trees, with forest animals running through it. Next to the forest on the left was a series of houses built in to the hills. The stone road they were standing on led to various shops that people were ducking in and out of. A group of ladies were outside a cafe chatting, while two men were wheeling a cart with a cage full of chickens. The air smelled fresh and clean, and when Benjamin breathed deeply his whole body warmed.

'These people look so relaxed,' Benjamin remarked as they walked along.

Opposite the trees was a big lake. The sun sparkled off the clear blue water. People swam in it, laughing. Others walked in the beautiful garden that circled it. Some were playing with the animals while others were talking amongst themselves.

Gideon nodded. 'They had no worries. Everything was provided for them and they took care of each other.'

'The tree!' Benjamin pointed to the far left. 'That's the tree in my dream.' Without waiting, he headed towards it. People and animals were eating the huge clumps of fruit that hung from it. It was the largest tree around, and seemed to be the one that everyone came to eat from. A stream ran close behind it, leading to a river that flowed along the border of Prysteen.

'Do you recognise that tree from somewhere other than your dream?' Gideon had come up behind him.

He looked at it closely. 'Is that the Vie tree? Is that the tree that I took the Earth league from the last time I was here?'

'It is indeed, but not how you saw it when you defeated the giant, Er. This is when the Vie tree was flourishing.'

'Wow. It's huge.' Benjamin noticed how it towered over even the tallest animal. For every fruit that was eaten, two grew back in its place.

Glancing over his shoulder, Benjamin did a double-take. 'Gideon, you're over there! How can you be over there – when you're here?'

Smiling, Gideon led the way towards himself. 'That was me in my youth.'

'But you don't look any different,' Benjamin remarked. 'How long ago did you say this was?'

'I've been around for a long time,' Gideon remarked. 'And I daresay I agree with you – I am quite unchanging.'

They approached the other Gideon, who was walking through the gardens with a man and a woman.

'Who are they?' Benjamin asked.

'Their names are Horatio and Helena Rivets. They are- or were – the governors of Prysteen.'

Gideon brought them alongside the three that were walking through the garden.

'Thank you for everything, Gideon,' said the man named Horatio. His long blonde hair blew in the gentle breeze.

'It makes me happy to see you enjoying Prysteen,' the young Gideon responded. 'As Governors of Prysteen, it is yours to oversee. All I ask is that you not cross the river.'

Horatio nodded his agreement, but the woman named Helena looked off in to the distance. 'But what about the places across the river? Who oversees them?'

'Everything past the river has been set aside for others. All you could possibly want or need is here in Prysteen.' The young Gideon fixed his eyes on Helena. 'You must not seek to cross the river. It is dangerous.'

Helena paused for a moment, her gaze lingering on the land far off. 'Of course,' she said eventually.

Benjamin saw a shadow go across the ground. He looked up but the sky was clear.

'I'd like to fast forward a bit now, Benjamin,' Gideon's voice startled him. 'Take my arm.' He hardly had time to grab Gideon's arm before a whirlwind of scenes came screaming past him. The ground under his feet shook as voices and images sped by him furiously.

It stopped as suddenly as it started, and they were once again standing in Prysteen. The long length of Helena's hair told Benjamin that some time has passed, and it was her that Gideon seemed interested in. She was alone now, wandering towards the river. The sun cast a dark shadow behind her.

'This way, Benjamin,' Gideon said, motioning to follow Helena.

She was sat on a flat stone by the river, watching the current. A hedgehog came out from the trees. Helena giggled and bent down to feed it some berries.

Sitting up, she startled at a strange man standing in front of her.

'Where did he come from?' Benjamin wondered aloud.

'Oh, hello Akness. I didn't hear you.' Helena addressed the man.

His slender body towered over her, a grin slid across his mouth. Long brown curls hugged his face.

'Sorry if I startled you,' said Akness, his dark brown eyes searching her.

'I was just admiring the river,' Helena turned back to the rushing water.

Akness followed her gaze. 'Shall we walk along it?'

She stood up and followed Akness. Gideon and Benjamin followed closely behind.

'Who is that man?' Benjamin asked.

Gideon put his index finger to his lips.

'So tell me, Helena,' Akness began. 'Did Gideon really say that you cannot be trusted to govern all of Meridia?'

'Gideon said that we must not cross the river, as we are the Governors of Prysteen.'

'Who is Gideon to decide who can and cannot cross the river?' There was an edge to Akness' voice Benjamin didn't like. 'And what of the rest of Meridia? They may be plotting against Prysteen, trying to take it for their own. Surely you and Horatio will need to be aware of any such plan.'

'Gideon has always said we are safe in Prysteen.'

'Helena, do you really believe one man could know all of that?' Akness said indignantly.

'Yes.' Helena responded quickly.

'Then are you not curious as to how Gideon got so clever? I have known Gideon for ages, and I am sure he is keeping something from you. Surely nothing will happen if you cross the river. It is shallow and look how far the land stretches on the other side.' Akness studied Helena intently.

Helena sighed deeply, her eyes gazing out past the river. 'Gideon said we are not to touch the water, or we would die.'

Akness took a step back. 'Die? What is this? There is no such thing while we have the Vie tree.' Akness caressed Helena's cheek. 'Gideon has said this to stop you crossing the river. He knows if you cross it, as he does, you will one day be as powerful as him.'

Helena turned to Akness. 'Is this true?'

He nodded. 'The river will give you strength, and you will be able to see the future.'

With only a moments' hesitation, Helena dipped her foot, followed by the other in to the river. She had waded out midway when she turned back to the bank. 'Akness you were right! Nothing bad has happened. And I feel stronger. I see with different eyes!' But Akness had gone in to the shadow of the trees.

'I'm not going to like what happens next, am I?' Benjamin asked Gideon. Gideon said nothing, tears in his eyes as he watched on.

'Akness?' Helena called out. Someone running towards her caught her attention. Scared at first, her face softened.

'Horatio, I'm glad it's you.'

Horatio stopped short. 'I got word that someone was in the river. Helena what are you doing? Don't you remember what Gideon said?'

'It's not true,' Helena answered. She began to swim around. 'Akness told me so. And the water is magical. Look, I can swim against the strongest current and my eyes can see wonderful things to come. You must come in with me, Horatio.'

Horatio cautiously approached the river's edge. With a glance over his shoulder, he walked straight in and waded over to Helena.

'Can you feel anything?' She asked her husband.

'Yes. I feel stronger. And I can – Helena, someone is coming.'

The two figures stood waist deep in the river, looking towards the sound. 'Hide,' Helena said and they both took a deep breath and submerged themselves.

'The river's going faster,' Benjamin said. He turned to Gideon who had moved to sit on a nearby rock, his head in his hands.

'This, my dear boy, is difficult for me to watch.'

77

From the path the young Gideon approached the river's edge. 'Horatio? Helena?'

After a moment the couple surfaced from under the water.

'What have you done?' Gideon asked.

The current was getting so strong the two struggled to stay standing.

'Helena convinced me to come in,' Horatio said, barely managing to get to shore.

'It was Akness,' Helena said defensively. She was splashing around now, struggling to keep her head above water as it rose. 'He – he told me – told me I could cross it.'

Helena's head went under twice. Both times it came up she gasped for air, her arms swinging above her. Her head went under again and did not come up. Horatio stood on shore, dripping wet, scanning the last spot Helena was seen.

'Helena! Helena!' He called out. He ran along the river bank, looking in to the rushing water that had risen to be almost level with the land. 'Helena! Please!' He dropped to his knees, searching.

After a few minutes passed Akness came sliding out from the shadows. 'She is dead,' he hissed.

Horatio stood up and looked from Akness to Gideon. 'Dead? What is this?'

Akness came closer. 'Gone,' he whispered. 'The life has drained out of her forever. She is gone.'

Dropping to his knees in front of Gideon, Horatio put his head in his hands. 'No,' he sobbed and looked at his hands in a confused state. He clutched his heart. 'What is this that I feel? Gideon, help me.'

Akness laughed. 'It is grief and shame, silly human. Helena is mine now, and so are you. And soon, all of Prysteen will be as well.'

'Silence.' Gideon's voice sent birds flying towards the sky. He turned to Akness. 'You have lied to these people. You are no longer to be known as Akness, but Howl is your name. Your wicked lies have caused this death. You think you have won but you are mistaken, you will never be able to claim Meridia. One day there will be one who will resist your lies and wicked ways, and you will lose.'

'I will build an army that will beat you Gideon,' Howl turned and disappeared in to the trees.

Gideon then turned to Horatio who was still sobbing at his feet. 'You had everything you could ever want and yet you wanted more. Now you know what death is and the Vie tree will soon die. You must leave this place and it will be destroyed. You will have to work hard for everything, and our friendship will never be the same again.'

With that, Gideon put his hands out in front of him and the earth started to tremble. With a mighty roar the river overflowed and flooded all of Prysteen. From the ground jagged, rocky mountains shot up, encircling Prysteen as people ran to safety.

7
The Sadness of Gideon

Once back at Water's Hyde, Benjamin and Gideon sat across from each other in silence.

'So that's how it all started?' Benjamin asked eventually.

'For the most part,' Gideon responded. His eyes shifted to the portrait that was once again on the wall, its landscape forever changing. 'Howl disguised himself as a friend to Helena and Horatio. They decided to trust him without thinking about what they were doing, and once they did-' his voice trailed off.

'Helena died.'

Gideon nodded, his face ashen. 'Howl used Helena's death to create Magh. Since he knew people could be deceived, he gave her control over building an army. Howl already had a quite a large following of Raptors. He made them submite to her. So she spread Raptors everywhere. Except for the very far north, there wasn't a town in Meridia that wasn't plagued by Raptors. Soon they were mixing with humans and a new breed was born.'

'A new breed?'

'Tattys,' Gideon responded. 'Half human, half Raptor. Gradually Magh's army got stronger and Howl

81

was able to sit back, letting Magh and his legions work to keep the scales unbalanced.' Gideon looked directly at Benjamin, his eyes sullen. 'Since you've managed to get the first league, Howl has become more involved and that means Magh as to work harder to try and stop you.'

The room was quiet for a few minutes, Benjamin's mind full of what he had just seen and heard. Gideon broke the silence. 'I think I will leave you to your thoughts. As always, please treat Water's Hyde as your home.'

Gideon disappeared down one of the corridors. After a while it occurred to Benjamin that he hadn't seen Hagar since he had been back. Hagar, the winged horse that lived in Gideon's back garden, had come to rescue him from the giant Er when he was last in Meridia getting the first of the four leagues. After a final glance at the portrait he got up and strode down the corridor that led to the back garden.

Sitting in a tree in the garden, he stroked Hagar's soft muzzle. There was so much to take in, he thought to himself, and they hadn't even started talking about the second league yet. He knew his job was to get all four leagues in the Arcrux to shift the balance of power back to where it was before. Over the years, Magh and her army had spread so much evil across Meridia that the scales shifted dangerously close to the world's collapse. Gideon had said before that time was on their side. But this trip to Meridia was different. It felt different. Like time was getting short. Like Magh was crouching at the door.

8

The Dreams of Benjamin Pringle

Benjamin spent most of his time with Hagar that week, until news came that Jeems and the rest were on their way back.

'I expect them back tonight,' Gideon confirmed. 'But it will be late and I suspect you will be asleep.' Winking as he walked away, Benjamin was left with the distinct impression that Gideon knew he would be unable to sleep.

Tucked away in the little back bedroom, he twisted restlessly in his soft bed. To distract himself he thought about Mr and Mrs Wink; how nice they were to him, the cosiness of their house and how it always smelled like freshly baked bread. It was awhile before he realised he was smiling at his thoughts. Fond memories turned in his mind until he fell asleep where different dreams found him.

Benjamin dreamed he was at Mrs Wink's house. Mr Wink was in the room saying something he couldn't understand. As he was talking, his mouth started changing. His teeth got sharp, his tongue big and thick and his neck started turning dark green. Benjamin ran down the corridor to find Mrs Wink, but was stopped by a bunch of furls that had sprung up in the corridor. He struggled passed and through a doorway that led straight in to Hadley Priest.

'Do we have any glue, Hester?' Riley asked as he came down the stairs towards him.

Suddenly Marcus ran in the house. 'Riley, quick, Motley's totally lost the plot!' Marcus scooped Riley up and ran out the front door. Benjamin turned and saw Motley. His eyes were totally black, smoke rose from under his collar. Fire burst from the palm of his right hand. He threw the fire at Benjamin. Out of nowhere Marcus threw himself between them, shielding Benjamin from the fireball.

'Benjamin! Go,' Marcus shouted. Then everything went silent.

Benjamin opened his eyes. He felt numb, unable to breathe right – like a heavy weight was on his chest pressing down. His guts churned noisily as he shook away sleepiness. It could not be possible, he thought, that surely would never happen. But some of his dreams had come true, hadn't they? Unable to quiet the voices in his head, he set out down the corridor to find Gideon.

He had only got half way down when he heard voices coming from the main room. He crept the rest of the way, stopping short of the entrance.

'I tell ya Gideon, Magh's comin' out in full force, so she is,' Jeems' voice was raspy and tired. 'She's way past furls an' the like,' he continued. 'Tatty's an' low level Raptors are crawlin' through them fields like red ants. It was nearly impossible ter get ourselves back 'ere.'

'He speaks the truth,' Taymar added. 'And our time spent with the Exiles does not bring good news. They fear they will be exposed soon.'

'What makes them think that?' Gideon asked.

'They think they have been betrayed,' responded Taymar.

'By who?'

'By one of their own people.'

Gideon broke the silence that followed. 'Then, whether from their own people or not, Magh is involved. She will do everything she can to please Howl, who I'm sure has not been happy with our progress.'

'How's Benjermin doin'?' Jeems asked.

'Full of thoughts, but fine,' Gideon answered. 'We have made good use of our time together.'

'Have ya told him about, ya know?'

'Jeems, if you are asking whether or not I discussed your past with Benjamin, the answer is no. But he did ask. The boy is very curious about what he heard the night he came to find you.

Jeems shifted uncomfortably and cleared his throat.

'The Benjamin I know is very forgiving,' Gideon continued. 'I think he will surprise you.'

'He has certainly surprised me,' Taymar added. 'Our little warrior is brave, although sometimes reckless! There is no doubt we will see great things from this child.'

On the other side of the wall, Primrose snorted inches away from Benjamin. He took a breath in sharply and jerked back in to the shadows as she sniffed the air towards him.

'Do ya think the Exiles will stay put?' Jeems asked Gideon.

Gideon was interrupted by Primrose, who snorted excitedly when her nose led her to Benjamin.

She pulled him out gently with her teeth and began licking him, her tongue hot against his skin.

'Stop it, Primrose. You're all smoky,' Benjamin laughed, turning his head to avoid her long, bright green tongue.

He saw Jeems first.

'Alright?' Benjamin asked.

'Right as rain,' Jeems responded.

'When did you guys get back?'

'Late last night,' said Taymar.

Benjamin furled his eyebrows. 'What time is it?'

'I'd say, judging how hungry I am, between breakfast and lunch,' Gideon replied.

'But,' he continued. 'Jeems and Taymar have not been awake long either, so,' he turned towards the fireplace, 'that means we can all have some breakfast.'

'Ya sleep okay, then?' Jeems stumbled over his words.

'Me?' Benjamin looked up. 'Uh, not bad. I've been up for awhile, just laying in bed,' he added quickly. His dream didn't seem as important anymore, given what he had just overheard.

'So where have you guys been?' He asked avoiding their gaze. He was sure they would be able to see right through him, how he had been listening at the door.

'Just sortin' things out is all,' Jeems replied as they all sat down at the table. Gideon was busy cooking, humming to himself with a grin on his face.

They all busied themselves with setting the table, Jeems trying his best to act natural.

'Are you ready for your next challenge, little warrior?' Taymar asked once they were sat down, a stack of raspberry pancakes in front of them.

'Um-mm,' Benjamin managed through a mouthful, melted butter and syrup running down his chin.

Gideon transferred some sausages onto a plate and put the pan back over the fire. 'By now you know that Magh, driven by Howl, has become increasingly desperate to stop you, Benjamin. There have been some obstacles, but nothing we couldn't get around.' He glanced over to Jeems who was concentrating on his food.

'So what do we do now?' Benjamin asked.

'The only thing we can do,' Gideon responded. 'Keep going.'

'Where's the next league?'

Taymar and Jeems exchanged a quick glance. 'That's the spirit of a true warrior,' Taymar remarked. Jeems nodded but didn't look up.

'You may not know this, Benjamin, but Meridia is a very big place indeed.' Gideon poured everyone a cup of tea. 'Its size has been a great advantage to me over the years, especially when I've had to find hiding places for people or things.' He chuckled. 'The next league is very far North where Meridia is covered in ice and snow.'

'I didn't bring my boots.'

Gideon raised his hand. 'As always, everything you need is here. As you can imagine the way is very different from before, and from what I've heard this morning, more difficult. I think it best that Jeems and Taymar let you know details as the days go on.'

'Why not now?'

'If you are captured, it is important that you know as little as possible about where we are going,' answered Taymar. 'Not that we will let that happen,' she added after a stern glance from Gideon.

It was silly, Benjamin realised later, to think that he would actually know what he was doing beforehand. It was also silly, he reasoned, to expect that they would be heading out right after they ate. As it turned out, Taymar and Jeems were exhausted from their trip, and Gideon insisted that they rest for a few days. 'Besides,' he added, 'I am sure that every Tatty in the land is looking for the two of you, so we will allow them time to get lazy again.'

The next three days passed quickly enough. Jeems was able to relax and soon he was back to normal. By mid-morning on day three they came out of Water's Hyde to a cold, overcast day ahead of them. The air was crisp and Benjamin breathed in deeply, the cold biting the inside of his nose. He hadn't realised how much he missed being outside.

They made their way to the river's edge where two rafts were laying in the foot of snow that covered the ground. They were sturdy enough, made out of ten logs strapped together, their bark stripped off, and the cracks plugged with what looked like a mixture of leaves and pine gum.

'Are we -' Benjamin pointed to the raft, a worried look on his face.

'We are,' finished Jeems. 'Yer not scared, are ya?'

'Er- no, it's just,'

'Mind,' Jeems interrupted. 'Yer not that great on the water.' He winked. 'Remember that Greenling wot got ya when we was goin' ter the Bogwumps? When we was on the way ter get the first league?'

'How could I forget?' He rubbed his shoulder where the Greenling had pierced it.

Primrose eyed the rafts nervously. She went to the rivers' edge and dipped her toe in the icy water, pulling it back quickly.

'Well o' course it's cold!' Jeems laughed. 'It's the middle o' the winter!' He pointed over her shoulder to where her raft was, fortified with extra large logs. 'Don' worry 'bout gettin' wet, I made yer raft good an' strong fer ya.'

Primrose crossed her arms and shook her head firmly. Jeems, who had been lowering one of the rafts in to the water, straightened up. 'Oh, so wot's this now? Eh? Are ya tryin' ter tell me that yer not comin' with us? Is that it?'

Primrose nodded with a smoky 'humph.'

'Well, okay,' Jeems said as he helped Benjamin load the packs onto Prinrose's raft. 'Stay 'ere if ya want. But just so ya know, Gideon's not goin' ter be around much, and with all them Bedruggers about.'

'Bedruggers?' Benjamin asked.

'Not now,' Jeems muttered out of the corner of his mouth.

Benjamin giggled, watching Primrose look from side to side along the river bank. She came over to her raft and inspected it, bobbing in the water. Jeems stopped what he was doing and stroked her snout. 'Ya'll be fine, girl. I wouldn't see ya get hurt, so I wouldn't.'

Taymar and Gideon, who had broken away to have a quiet word, were making their way to the edge of the river.

'We shall have to keep away from the shore,' Taymar said to Jeems, who nodded his agreement.

Gideon waited for Benjamin to finish loading the raft. 'I trust you still have everything I gave you on your last visit to Meridia.'

Benjamin nodded. 'Rope's in my pack.' He had his staff in his hand and patted his left trouser pocket, the small stone with the oracle safely inside. 'And this,' he said, fishing the Arcrux from around his neck.

Gideon stopped him. 'Thank you, Benjamin. As important as it was to keep the Arcrux hidden during your last adventure, it is even more important now. Magh is looking for you, and has got most of her army out.' Gideon gave him a stern look. 'But I suspect you would know that when you are listening in corridors to conversations that don't involve you.'

'Sorry,' Benjamin looked at the ground.

'It's quite alright. It is in your nature to be curious.'

Gideon smiled. Benjamin responded with a quizzical look. He couldn't help but feel slightly annoyed. How could Gideon say that it didn't involve him? When Jeems and Taymar came back, that's all they were talking about. Why shouldn't he know everything there was to know? Wasn't he the one that had to fight Magh and get the leagues? The sound of a raft sloshing around in the water distracted Benjamin from his thoughts.

'Primrose, calm down and ya won't get wet,' Jeems hollered. The little dragon rocked back and forth on her raft, struggling to keep her balance. Water splashed up and over the secured packs.

'Jeems, you can travel with your dragon,' Taymar said as she strode past Benjamin to the shore. 'We won't need three rafts.' 'Little warrior, you and I can share this one.'

Benjamin helped Taymar get their raft in to the water. As they sailed downstream, he looked from

Gideon who was standing onshore, to the other raft where Jeems was still struggling with Primrose.

'Your friends will not stray from us, little warrior,' Taymar said. 'It is better this way. Only Jeems can calm Primrose when she is anxious.' Taymar guided the raft along with an long, thick branch. She looked over her shoulder to Primrose and Jeems. 'I think we will have a much smoother ride,' she chortled.

Jeems was trying to keep the raft straight while Primrose moved from side to side, her nose close to the water. 'Don't ya even *think* 'bout fishin',' Jeems ordered. 'Yer gonna capsize us, so ya will. And besides, ya've had enough ter eat. Now sit still.' Benjamin chuckled and faced the front, trying not to feel the cold.

Everything was quiet and still along the river. Hills dotted the fields on either side, the odd patch of grass poking through the snow. The forest was off in the distance behind them to the left, and the Bogwump cloud way off to the right.

'I hope the Bogwumps are okay.'

Taymar steered around a rock. 'You have seen how they are protected. They are fine for the moment.' Benjamin watched the cloud until they drifted around a bend in the river. 'We need to look ahead, little warrior, but I would be surprised if you did not see the Bogwumps again.'

He sat in silence, thinking about when he met the Bogwumps the last time he was in Meridia. He thought back to his Raising Ceremony and Thuglot, the Bogwump chief. 'It's pretty cool though, isn't it? To be able to tell the future like that, like the Bogwumps can.'

Taymar nodded. 'I suppose 'cool' is a more human word, but yes, the gift of foresight is very powerful. And that is why the Bogwumps are so heavily protected. It must be used the right way. It can be dangerous if used for the wrong reasons.'

'I thought they were supposed to tell people the future.'

Taymar shook her head. 'Not always. The Bogwumps both encourage and warn people of what is to come. Sometimes an oracle can be used to help someone who is heading down the wrong path, and sometimes it is to encourage those who are on the right one.'

Benjamin looked off in to the distance, a bit confused with what Taymar was saying. He had already decided that she was slightly odd, and more confusing than Gideon. He listened to her humming and singing softly in her strange language. It was a while before he spoke again.

'Are those houses?' Benjamin asked, studying the burned remains of a small group of stone structures coming up along the right side of the river. They were barely discernable amongst the black ash and charred wood. Little black mounds were littered further away from the river, following what looked like a path that had overgrown with thistles and other weeds.

'It used to be a village where people lived,' Taymar answered without looking.

'Oh.' Benjamin thought for a moment. 'How did it burn down?'

'Like most of the them,' Taymar responded.

Benjamin sat silently, trying to figure out what she meant without wanting to ask. Taymar continued. 'That village is just one of the many that were built along the shores of the river. There were many more throughout these fields.'

'Oh yeah, I remember Gideon had an old map that I was looking at. He said something about villages being all over the place.'

Taymar suddenly seemed more watchful. She eyed the burnt buildings suspiciously as they drifted passed.

'So, how did they burn down?' Benjamin chanced another question.

'Bedruggers and Tatty's invaded all of the villages, one after another.'

'Huh?'

'Two groups who are part of the Legions of the Damned. The group run by Howl and his deputy, Magh.'

'Wha-' Benjamin did not have time to finish his question before Taymar put her finger to her mouth and crouched down. She was focused on a group of derelict houses that were up ahead on the left side of the river. Jeems too was on all fours, looking in the same direction but Primrose, Benjamin was relieved to see, was more interested in dragging her claws in the water in hopes of snagging a fish.

As they got closer, Benjamin realised what all the fuss was about. They had company.

9

Bad Company

In her crouching position, Taymar made an odd hand gesture to Jeems, who nodded his agreement. They approached the group of houses silently, the river inching them forward. Murmured voices came from the rabble. The rafts were directed to the opposite side of the widened river, all eyes on the group of houses as they drifted past.

'Who's in there?' Benjamin's voice was barely audible.

Taymar just shook her head, not taking her eyes off the burnt mounds until they were safely around the next bend. Once out of earshot, Taymar and Jeems brought the rafts to shore and silently began untying the packs. As they were getting off, Taymar motioned towards two huge boulders that jutted from the ground about twenty feet inward. Quickly and quietly, packs were transferred from the rafts to their hiding place behind the rocks. Taymar hurried Benjamin along, as Jeems did with Primrose, who was not at all impressed about leaving fresh fish behind.

'They have started occupying their old hideouts,' Taymar whispered to Jeems.

'Who?' Benjamin asked.

Jeems nodded. 'They're onter us, make no mistake. Question is, wot do we do now?'

'Who's on to us?'

Taymar gripped the handle of her sword. 'I could deal with them swiftly.'

'What? Is it Magh?'

'Nah,' Jeems shook his head. 'It's way too early fer that. We'll be sniffed out, so we will.'

'Hello!'

Shocked, Jeems and Taymar turned to Benjamin.

'Thank you,' he sighed. 'Now that I have your attention, what's happening?'

'Those voices we heard we some o' Magh's men, so they were,' Jeems answered. 'Bedruggers, more'n likely.' He turned to Taymar, 'We need ter find a different way across Meridia. We're sittin' ducks here in the river.'

Taymar nodded. 'Well, unless the two of you can grow wings,' he chortled, 'we are limited to going across land.'

'I wonder,' Jeems muttered thoughtfully, looking around.

'What?' Benjamin risked talking.

'It's just,' Jeems began crawling inland. 'In the days when things were gettin' bad, we - I mean, they had ter find ways of creepin' up on people. So Magh had 'er Bedruggers dig trenches along the river so they could ambush folk.'

Jeems crawled steadily inland, patting the overgrown grass every so often. 'It could be,' he continued, 'that one o' them trenches is still around 'ere, seein' as we're not far from them houses.'

'But that would've been ages ago,' Benjamin was hushed by Taymar. 'I mean,' he whispered, 'wouldn't they be filled in by now?'

'Not necessarily,' Taymar answered. 'Now hush, little warrior. We are at risk of being caught and I would like to avoid a battle right now if it can be helped.'

Both turned back to Jeems who was shaking his head. 'It don't look like it,' he started, 'it would've bin 'round -' his voice trailed off and he disappeared in to the ground.

They darted after him. When they reached the spot where Jeems had vanished, they found him in a trench that was dug about six feet in to the ground.

'This will do nicely,' Taymar said with a smile on her face.

Jeems brushed himself off. 'I can't say fer sure how far it goes, but it'll take us in the right direction.' He put his hand out for Taymar to help him up. 'I'll give ya a hand with the packs and then we should be headin' out. Summon'll notice them rafts soon and then we'll be in fer it if we don't get in ter these trenches.'

'Wait a minute, though, don't you think they'll be using them again?'

'Nah,' Jeems brushed his hands together. 'They wouldn't need them anymore, would they? There's no need fer them ter sneak up on folk 'cos there's no'un ter sneak up on. We shouldn't meet up with anyone. Well, fer now, anyways.'

Swiftly and silently the three managed to get the packs in to the trench where Primrose sat sulking. 'Yer too big ter help,' Jeems had quipped. 'And loud. Yer best down 'ere an' out o' the way.'

By the time they were ready to head in to the trench, it was getting quite dark. 'It must be late,'

Benjamin said aloud, hoping for a suggestion of dinner to follow.

'You must remember we are in the middle of winter, little warrior,' Taymar answered. 'It is only late in the afternoon.'

'We'll make a start, anyways, before we stop an' grab a bite ter eat.' Jeems added. 'Primrose, ya'll have ter walk on all fours.' Stuck out at least a foot over the top of the trench, Primrose gave a loud *humph*, a ring of smoke floating up from out of her nose.

'Well then ya might as well bawl fer all yer worth, yer that obvious!' Jeems dropped his arms to either side of him. 'I knows ya don't like crawlin', but there's no choice, so there isn't. For a little dragon, yer still too big fer this 'ere trench.'

Primrose scowled and fell onto her hands.

'Right,' Jeems turned his attention to Benjamin and Taymar. 'I don't think we'll have any problems in this 'ere trench, but all the same, we need ter be on our guard.'

The night was silent, save for the now faraway sounds of laughing coming from the houses they passed earlier. The trench was littered with weeds and roots making it tricky to manoeuvre around without getting caught up. Every time Benjamin tripped over a root he protested louder until Jeems produced a small torch from his pack.

''ere ya go,' he said kindly. 'Just try ter keep it pointed ter the ground.'

Benjamin nodded and started walking again, comforted at Jeems' kindness. Although he would have rather been talking and laughing with his friend, the silence gave him some time to think. Magh had obviously gotten more active and that made things more stressful. Then again, he reasoned, he didn't really know what he was doing the last time he was here, it was just such a blur. His mind turned to Motley. Although he still didn't really know where Motley fitted in, he knew it wasn't good. He pushed away fear and guilt when he thought of Marcus and Riley at Hadley Priest, none the wiser about how evil Motley really was.

They walked for a few hours, Benjamin's feet sore from stubbing his toes repeatedly. 'Do you think we've gone far enough?'

'If I remember right, there's a little bunker just up ahead,' Jeems whispered. A short time later they came up to three large holes that had been dug in the sides of the wall. The trench had widened up in that area, with extra brush covering it above.

'They have these bunkers along all the trenches,' Jeems told Benjamin as they unpacked some food. 'Ter do just what we're doin' now – spend the night or grab a kip.' He pointed upwards. 'They would always make sure there was extra brush up top an' all. They're master hiders.'

'Gideon was right, you do know everything about Meridia.'

Jeems got sadly quiet, rummaging around for another plate. 'Learnt most of it the hard way,' he muttered.

Taymar broke the awkward silence that followed. 'Come, little warrior, and tell me all about your friends at Hadley Priest.'

Benjamin chatted happily to Taymar while Jeems used Primrose to heat up some sausages. 'Made 'em meself,' Jeems declared proudly after compliments about dinner. The three ate and talked for quite a while, mostly about everything except the dangers around them. After dinner they got their bedrolls out and nestled in to one of the wide ledges that were carved in the trench walls. Primrose lay on the ground between them, snoring and twitching. Jeems and Benjamin laughed at her as she started to run in her sleep and whimper.

'Bad dream,' Jeems whispered from his bunker. 'She gets 'em every now an' again. I reckon it's from when she was little.'

'Oh?' Benjamin said.

Jeems sighed. 'I'll tell ya some other time. Get some sleep.'

The bunker was small, making it slightly uncomfortable. Benjamin shifted restlessly for ages, worrying about Riley and Marcus before drifting off to sleep.

He dreamed that he was running through the forest towards Jeems, who was swinging high over a scorching fire. Suddenly someone caught Benjamin by the arm. He turned around and Motley was standing behind him, Riley's glasses in his hands.

The scene changed.

He was standing in the trench, tree roots wrapping themselves around him. Jeems was looking at him and laughing. He struggled free and climbed out, colliding with Magh.

Benjamin opened his eyes to deep darkness. He stared up at the midnight sky, peppered with stars. Every sound made him jump, his teeth chattering from the cold. A shadow passed over and he pulled his bedroll to his chin. Footsteps on the ground above.

Fighting against it, his mind turned to random thoughts. Marcus and Riley at home; Huxley Boyd, the bully at school.

He fell in to another dream.

In an underground chamber, he was facing two tunnels. Three snakes slithered up from behind him, coiling around his feet before passing under his legs. Two of them twisted together like a rope and went down the tunnel to the left. The third snake stayed coiling and uncoiling itself around his ankles. From one of the tunnels he heard his name, 'Benjamin, Benjamin.'

'Benjermin, Benjermin. Wake up,' Jeems' hoarse voice filtered through his dream.

'Huh?' Benjamin jumped violently at the sight of Jeems.

'Wot r-' Jeems stopped, bewildered.

It took Benjamin a minute to recover. 'Sorry. I was having a bad, well a weird, well,' He sighed heavily. 'I was having a crazy dream.'

'Right,' Jeems nodded slowly. 'We need ter get movin'.'

'But it's the middle of the night,' Benjamin protested, struggling to get out of his bedroll.

'Just comin' ter day break,' Jeems corrected, helping Benjamin with is pack. 'An' keep yer voice down, ya never know wot's out there.'

'I thought I heard footsteps earlier, before I fell back to sleep.'

'All the more reason ter get movin'.' Jeems tightened the straps on his own pack. 'Taymar an' Primrose have already left so we'll have ter catch them up.'

After about ten minutes of trotting behind Jeems, Benjamin saw the two others up ahead. He stumbled along sleepily, his latest dream swirling around his head.

'Jeems?' Benjamin called out.

'Right 'ere,' Jeems answered. 'It's comin' ter daylight now, ya should be able ter see me.'

Benjamin ignored the comment. 'When will we be seeing Gideon again?'

Jeems walked along for a few minutes before answering. He looked at the rising sun. 'I reckon it won't be long.'

The sun warmed Benjamin's face, giving a wave of comfort. Taymar had climbed out of the trench to scout around, and once she gave the all clear they followed her out, ducking in to a group of trees nearby, the river still on their left.

'Is this the best place to try and cross the river?' Taymar asked Jeems when they had settled between three huge trees that were twisted together.

'Not the safest, but the best chance of actually gettin' across.' Jeems unpacked some food and everyone helped themselves.

'Where's the safest? Oh, sorry Primrose,' Benjamin scooped up the bits of apple he sprayed all over the little dragon.

'Up ahead a few miles. But it's loaded with screaming stones,' Jeems answered. 'There's only one way ter get across them stones, so there is, and there ain't no time ter teach ya the code. So,' Jeems nodded towards the river, 'this 'ere's the best way. Ya just gotta be careful is all.'

'Is it deep?' Benjamin asked. 'It's just,' his voice dropped. 'I can't swim.'

'It'd be up ter about yer chest, I'd say,' Jeems measured him with his eyes then smiled. 'Ha! Ya've grown an' all since ya've bin here last.' Jeems threw some food over to Primrose who turned her nose up at it. 'It's just the current is strong – real strong. Ya'll have ter hold on ter me or Taymar. Or we'll tow ya. I suppose that'll be the best way.'

Benjamin was just about to ask if there was anything dangerous in the river when Jeems launched in to Primrose. 'Don't ya bother turnin' yer nose up at that food, ol' girl. I can't tell ya when we're gonna get the chance ter eat again, dragon, so eat up!'

Taymar laughed softly and shook her head. 'Come, little warrior,' she said as she packed up. 'I suspect we are being followed, and you can't stay in one place for too long when you are the hunted.' She quickly packed up her stuff and led the way out towards the river. Benjamin went out after her, looking over his shoulder to check on Jeems who was trying to coax Primrose to eat. When they got to the water's edge, Benjamin noticed that the river was narrow but the current was strong. The clear water exposed four large, flat stones along the bottom of the river straight to the other side. They were covered in a layer of green scum, the grass around them waving viciously.

'They look slippery.'

Taymar nodded. 'It will be too risky to use them, as tempting as they might be. If we fall off the current will surely drag us under.' She paused a moment to think. 'We'll have to wade through,' she motioned to Jeems who had come up behind them with Primrose.

'If ya get yer rope out, Benjermin, we'll tow ya across,' he suggested. Benjamin dropped his pack to the ground and rifled through it. He kept one eye on Taymar, who was already in the water. A few steps in and it was up to her waist. She struggled against the current, losing her balance once, but catching herself before her head went under. Once on the other side, she got out quickly, looking around, her hand on the hilt of her sword.

He handed the rope to Jeems who unravelled it and passed him one end. 'Awright, I'll go next. Wait 'til I'm on the other side before ya start crossin' cos I'm gonna try an' wrap this 'ere end around a tree. An' watch where I'm walkin', it may help ya ter know whereabouts ter step.'

'Okay.' Primrose's wing brushed his hair has she heaved herself up and flew low over the water.

'Keep close, Primrose,' Benjamin said after her.

'Don't worry 'bout her,' Jeems called out as he waded in to the river. 'She's not goin' anywheres. She's more scared than you are at the minute.'

'I don't think so,' Benjamin said under his breath. He looked up to the storm clouds that were moving in, dark and uninviting. 'Awright Benjermin,' Jeems called out after he was across, wet through up to his neck and shivering fiercely.

He waited until Jeems had the rope securely tied around the closest tree before he stepped towards the water. Stamping his feet in an effort to warm them up, he waded in. The current was even stronger than it looked from the shore, and he immediately struggled to stay upright. Then the drop off and he was suddenly up to his chest, icy water splashing on his face. He gripped the rope, letting Jeems and Taymar pull him across while his feet slipped along the river floor.

'Tie it 'round yer waist,' Jeems hollered, 'in case ya lose yer grip.' Benjamin nodded and managed to steady himself against one of the large, flat stones. The current whipped the long grass around his ankles, causing him to stumble.

'Hang on Benjermin, I'll come an' get ya,' Jeems urged.

'I can do it,' he retorted, splashing about. Recovering, he fumbled with the rope, trying to get it around himself without going under. The clouds above were now heavy and low, a loud clap of thunder echoed through the air.

'It's gonna rain, so it is. I'll come get ya.'

'I've got it,' Benjamin persisted.

'This ain't no time ter play hero!' Jeems called out.

Jeems dropped the rope and headed down the bank. Annoyed, Benjamin shifted his weight too much and the undercurrent swept his feet out from under him. He felt the rope slip from his hands as he was dragged under, bouncing off the bottom of the river, racing with the current. His feet searched for ground, his hand searching for something to grip until he finally managed to get his head above water. He was up long enough to see Taymar and Jeems running alongside him on the shore, shouting. He managed a quick breath before the current pulled him down again, this time hitting his head on a large log that was embedded in the thick mud. Blood poured from the gash it caused. He resurfaced and tried to focus.

'Awww,' Primrose bawled from the shore.

'Gideon!' Benjamin managed before going under once more.

Try as he might, he was no match for the strong current and cross currents. He floated freely for a time before he was able to get his feet under him, but he had been swept in to the deepest part of the river and was unable to feel bottom.

Struggling, he drifted swiftly down the river, the current pressing him under. Suddenly his foot caught something solid, and his knees crashed in to the river bank. With his last ounce of strength, he dug his fingers in to the muddy bank until his hands wrapped around a bunch of strong roots and he thrust his head out of the water. He looked to his right and noticed a low lying branch a few feet ahead of him. He reached up, grabbed ahold of it and pulled himself to shore.

'Taymar, he's out! Up ahead on the other side.' Benjamin could barely hear Jeems over the rushing river. Thunder clapped loudly and rain poured down. He scrambled up the bank laying in mud and snow, panting.

'Benjermin, ya've got ter go up ahead a bit where the river gets shallow,' Jeems called from the other side.

Nodding, he slowly got up and stumbled along the river until he came to a spot where the water was just above his ankles. Seven large flat stones with markings on them lay in a path to the other side. He jumped on the first stone at the same time Jeems called out.

Suddenly an ear piercing scream ripped through the air. Benjamin scrambled back to shore, his hands over his ears.

'Them's screaming stones,' Jeems yelled over. 'Ya'll have ter go up a bit. I can't get over ter ya from here 'cause this is a one way crossing.'

'What?' Benjamin couldn't hear Jeems over the screaming, but it didn't matter now. From the trees on the other side of the river, a group of rough looking men swinging chains and small tree trunks advanced towards them. They raced towards Taymar and Jeems, who started fighting them off.

'Look out on yer side,' Jeems managed to call out while fighting off two men. Way down the river on Benjamin's left were two men coming towards him.

'What now?' Benjamin asked frantically.

'Yer're gonna have to try and get across,' Taymar answered. 'Try and work out the symbols.'

'What symbols?' Benjamin asked, looking around.

'The ones on the screaming stones,' Jeems eventually answered. He ducked under a left hook and jumped over a large piece of wood. 'And on the tree behind ya.'

Benjamin whipped around and scanned the trees that lined the riverbank. His eyes rested on a particularly small tree set in the middle of two very large ones. The bark on the front had been scrapped away, and Benjamin could see oddly shaped scratches. When he got closer he realised that he had seen them somewhere before.

But from where? He desperately tried to remember if it was in a dream. Then it occurred to him – Marcus!

'It's Marcus' code!' Remembering his last day at Hadley Priest, he padded his trouser pocket and felt a soggy ball of paper. He pulled out the last note Marcus had passed him before coming back to Meridia. Frantic to peel it open, he tore the drenched paper in two.

'Ahh,' he growled. Piecing it together, he compared the symbols on the note to the one on the tree. They were an exact match.

He turned around excitedly. 'Jeems! I know the code!'

'Good. Now use it!' Jeems barked back. Between fighting, Taymar threw her boomerang at the men after Benjamin. Catching them both at the knees, they tumbled in to the river.

Benjamin turned back to the tree. He never had to read any of Marcus' notes under pressure, and most of the time he always had the guide book handy. It then occurred to him that he hadn't even had the chance before now to read this note. When Marcus gave it to him he had just shoved it in his pocket and forgot about it.

Recalling the alphabet and symbols, he slowly started reading the note aloud:

Now you know why I made you learn this code. You will need this to get across the screaming stones. Don't go mental now. Tell you everything when I see you. Marcus.

His felt his stomach drop. Marcus knew about Meridia. How could it be? And why didn't he tell anyone?

'You must come now little warrior,' Taymar called from across the river.

Shaking it out of his mind, he raced back to the water. Two more men were approaching on his side, but on the other side Taymar was taking care of the last man with her sword. Jeems was busy trying to calm Primrose, who was bawling and running in circles with her eyes closed.

'Right.' He returned to the torn note in his hand.

Stones are numbered from 1-9:

Right foot on number 1

Finding the symbols on the stones was easy, but they were in a strange order. The stone with the *1* on it wasn't the closest to the riverbank, so he had to stretch out his right leg, balancing himself on the correct one. The screaming stopped instantly, but the rocks were slippery and the icy rain was making it difficult to see. He could hear the men hollering at him, getting closer.

Left foot on number 2

He put his left foot on the stone that was closest to shore. Straddling the stones, carefully balancing against the rushing water, he read the next step.

Right foot on number 3.

The stone directly in front of him read number 4.

'Benjermin hurry up, ya got some bedruggers behind ya,' Jeems sounded slightly closer.

'I can't find number 3!'

'Over there, ter the left of ya,' Jeems called back.

'I see it!' He jumped, his right foot landing squarely on the stone.

Left foot on number 4.

'How am I suppose to do that?'

'Just do it!' Jeems shot back. 'And watch out behind ya!'

Benjamin turned to see one of the bedruggers jump on stone number 2 and the ear piercing scream came back. He jumped back, colliding with his partner.

Benjamin twisted his body around, planting his left foot on stone number 4.

'You're not going anywhere fast,' one of the bedruggers growled. He was now on the first rock. 'There's too much money on your head for me to be worried about a few screaming stones.'

The rain was turning in to sleet, and the ice pricked his skin like pins. Quickly Benjamin looked at the note again.

Skip number five. Both feet on number six

Taking his left foot off of the furthest stone, he balanced on his right leg for a moment. A splash from behind threw him off balance and he wobbled slightly. As the bedruggers jumped randomly, the stones were trying to shake them off.

'Get on the next stone and then you'll be out of the way of the bedruggers,' Taymar coaxed.

He heaved himself the few feet to the next stone and looked back. The first bedrugger had been taken by the river but the second one had made it back to shore and was throwing rocks at him.

'Ow!'

A rock hit his leg hard. Wobbling, he read the last instruction.

Right foot on number 7. Left foot on shore.

He nearly missed the last stone, his left foot skimming the icy water. Jeems clasped his hand and they tumbled to shore.

'We've gotta get outta here,' Jeems said over and over again.

They ran for at least twenty minutes, weaving through trees, stopping occasionally to listen for anyone following them. They continued on in the now raging sleet until they reached an abandoned old barn in an open field on the edge of a dirt road.

'What do we do now?' Benjamin panted, doubled over.

'Keep yer voice down,' Jeems whispered after him. 'We're not outta danger yet, not by a long shot.'

Benjamin stood by Primrose while Jeems and Taymar peered through the slats of the old barn. As scared as Benjamin had ever seen her, the little dragon held her breath, fearing a bout of hiccups as she had become so frightened. Straw littered the dirt floor of the old barn. A rusty pitchfork was stabbed in to a bale of musty smelling hay along the back wall. In the far corner there were a few rusty buckets and a chain that ran up and over a pulley to a high loft.

Benjamin found a dry spot in the corner and collapsed, his mind stuck on Marcus. How did he know about Meridia? And that code - Marcus said he had made that code up himself, but obviously not.

'Jeems?' The sleet shattered against the tin roof of the leaky barn. He shivered, watching his friend talking to Taymar in a corner.

'J-Jeems.'

Jeems looked up. 'None of this is makin' any sense ter ya, is it?' He asked softly as he came over.

He pulled his bedroll out and wrapped it around Benjamin.

His body shaking uncontrollably, all Benjamin shook his head. After a long pause, he found his voice. 'That c-code, the one that was on the s-stones.'

Jeems nodded.

'My friend M-Marcus made that code up. Th-that's what he told me, anyways.' Benjamin stopped for a minute, the cold getting the better of him. 'But that can't be, can it? B-because how could it be the same? I don't – I just don't get it.' He sank in to the bedroll.

'There's lots of what goes on in Meridia that don't make sense ter me either,' Jeems said quietly. 'Some of it makes me crazy, some of it seems not too bad, and some of it I just can't think about 'cause I'll end up seein' chickens.'

Benjamin's chest heaved with a sullen laugh.

'But I'm sure that if summat's happened here that has helped ya, or kept ya safe, like Marcus knowin' the code ter the screamin' stones, fer instance, then Gideon's involved somehow.' Jeems held his hand up to stop Benjamin from interrupting. 'Now I'm not sayin' I know the answers ter yer quandaries, but I am sayin' that if it's fer good, and if it's doin' ya good, then it's Gideon. It's gotta be. He's loves ya too much fer it ter be otherwise.'

Benjamin sighed deeply. 'I guess love is weird.'

'It's not fer the faint-hearted,' Jeems chuckled. 'I reckon we'll be seein' Gideon before long. Ya may want ter have a chat with him 'bout everything.'

Benjamin nodded. 'Jeems?'

'Yep.'

'I've been having dreams, strange dreams. Sometimes I dream about something and then it happens.'

Jeems raised his eyebrows.

'Not all the time, and not every dream. But sometimes I'll dream about something or someone or I'll see something in my dream that I've never seen before and then I'll see it a few days later or something.'

Jeems shrugged. 'Well, ya'll certainly have ter talk ter Gideon then. Sounds like yer dreams are tryin' ter tell ya things. Maybe even tryin' ter warn ya of stuff before it happens. I'm not sure I'm the best one ter tell ya 'bout all of that.'

'How did I know you were going to say that?'

'Keep yer mind off it fer the time bein' and see wot Primrose is up ter.' Jeems winked, got up with a grunt and went over to where Taymar was keeping watch.

'Reckon there's a few more of 'em since we were last 'round here,' Benjamin overheard Jeems say to Taymar.

Taymar nodded. 'They will find us eventually, no matter how quiet or quick we thought we were. Shall I go and see if we've been followed?' Jeems nodded and she ducked out of the barn in to the frozen rain.

There was silence again in the barn save for the sound of Primrose scratching through the musty straw and the constant tapping of ice against tin.

'Yer a right gut, ya are Primrose,' Jeems teased. 'I told ya we wouldn't be eatin' fer a while, but did ya listen ter me – nooo. An' yer not goin' huntin' so don't ask.' The little dragon scowled and plunked herself down next to Benjamin.

'Don't mind her,' Jeems continued. 'She gets grumpy when she's hungry.'

Benjamin stroked Primrose's snout until her eyes started to close.

Sleet turned to snow as they waited in the barn, lost in their own thoughts. Daylight was almost over when Taymar finally came running across the field.

'It is as we feared,' she reported once inside. 'The road is being watched. It is of little use for us to try and get to the league this way.' Her eyes met Jeems who started to shake his head. He led her in to the far corner.

'I know wot yer thinkin', Taymar, so I do,' he kept his voice low. 'But I'm not so sure it's a grand idea. Not from wot I saw when we was last there. Ol' Hubrice will have his back up, so he will an' I'm not sure we should take the risk, 'specially if them rumours are true.'

'But our choices are limited,' Taymar argued. 'We cannot linger here much longer.'

'I agree we're sittin' ducks right now,' Jeems responded, 'but wot if we're leadin' him from the fryin' pan in ter the fire so ter speak.'

Out of the corner of his eye, Benjamin saw Taymar look over to him. He stroked Primrose and closed his eyes.

'Even if there is a traitor amongst them,' she turned back to Jeems. 'The chamber is heavily protected. And do not forget Mrs Peabody.'

'Who's Mrs Peabody?' Benjamin piped up.

'I thought you was goin' ter sleep with Primrose,' Jeems said gruffly.

Benjamin looked down at the sleeping dragon, then stood up. 'If you're talking about me I should know. You don't have to protect me. I know that Magh wants me dead. Even if Gideon hadn't told me I think I would have figured it out by now anyways.

What did you think was happening when I was trying to cross the river? Or the last time I was in Meridia, when I fell over the cliff with Khor, or was getting crushed by Er? I may be just a kid to you, but I'm a kid that's doing something not every kid does, and that makes me different. Most kids live with their parents, not some dumpy children's home-.' His voice trailed off and the barn was silent.

'Right you are, little warrior,' Taymar finally responded. 'And we were wrong to discount you. But I fear we have wasted time so if you can trust us, we will tell you more when we get to the protection of Mrs Peabody's house.'

Benjamin nodded stiffly. He looked out to the road that ran in front of the barn. Across it was a stone bridge that arched over a path through the snowy grass. The bridge held an old railway track that hadn't been used for a long time. The tracks ended a few feet past the bridge to a mound of dirt overgrown with grass and brush, covered with snow.

Taymar looked out cautiously before she led the way out of the barn and across the road. Jeems said goodbye to Primrose, who, he explained, was too big to try and sneak around. Promising he would come back for her as soon as the coast was clear, he followed Benjamin out of the barn. Taymar led them quietly across the road, stopping under the bridge. Benjamin sighed deeply but was hushed when Jeems pointed out two men in a tree not far from them through the archway.

'Who are they?' Benjamin whispered.

'Bedruggers, looks like,' Jeems answered.

'What are they doing up there?'

'Watchin' Mrs Peabody's house,' Jeems said, pointing to the far right.

It was the first time Benjamin noticed the house nestled in the bottom of the hill below the train tracks. It was pretty and well kept, with a dark green fence around the sides and front. The thatched roof looked new and the white paint that covered the house was bright and cheery. The front garden was full of high plants and flowers, with bordering shrubs following each other up to the black door. Despite snow all around, Mrs Peabody's garden looked beautiful.

'How are we going to get passed them?'

Taymar motioned for them to follow her, and they silently set out through the tall grass to the left and behind the bedruggers. In ankle-deep snow they walked a huge semi-circle around the back of the tree, and then cut in, heading straight for them. They stopped every time one of the bedruggers looked their way, and the sun was starting to set by the time they managed to squeeze behind a pile of dirt. The three of them peered out from their hiding place, resting on their elbows, trying to figure out their next move.

'They need distractin', they do,' Jeems decided and picked up a rock from the mound in front of them.

He got to his knees and fired the rock at the men, hitting one in the back of the head.

'Oi, what did you do that for?' Asked the one with spiky black hair, rubbing his head.

'Do what?' Asked his friend with long greasy hair.

'Don't give me that, Pyrit. You knows what you did.'

'I don't know what you're on about,' the man named Pyrit answered. He sniffed up, his left nostril of his long nose crinkling.

'You elbowed the back of me head.'

Pyrit shook his head. 'Hawke, if I elbowed your head, you'd be knocked off this tree.'

'You did something,' the one named Hawke grumbled.

'You've been watching this house too long,' said Pyrit as he looked around.

'Oh, and you're all brains, are ya,' Hawke said roughly.

'Well, at least I'm not hallucinating,' Pyrit said. 'Wouldn't look too good, would it, if you went back to base claiming things were happening that weren't. Some might say you was losing your mind.'

Hawke stood up, balancing on the thick branch. 'Who says I'm losing me mind? I know you did something behind me back.' Hawke glared at Pyrit who sat casually. 'Look at you, sitting there all smug. Nah, the only one losing anything here is you,' Hawke said as he put his foot to Pyrit's back.

Pyrit wobbled, waving his arms in a desperate attempt to rebalance himself. Giving up, he managed to grab hold of Hawke's left leg, bringing them both down to the ground.

They stood up, locked in battle.

'Okay,' said Jeems, 'this 'ere's our chance.'

They crawled as fast as they could around the bedruggers, who were throwing punches and shouting at each other. Benjamin looked back twice, but they showed no signs of noticing the trespassers. Now and then one or the other would yell 'ouch,' or 'why you-.' Benjamin chortled. 'If all bedruggers are this dim, getting to the league should be easy.'

'Don't get too comfy,' Jeems shot back. 'There's lots o' them out there, an' they ain't all that dim.'

They continued crawling through the snow until they reached the tall cedar trees that lined the path up to the little house. Once behind the trees, they got up and waited for Jeems to collect Primrose.

'Finally,' Benjamin said when they came in to sight. He blew on his hands and rubbed them together. 'I'm freezing.'

'We still need to get through the door, but we are heavily guarded,' Taymar responded. Benjamin followed along, unsure of what she meant. Not far down the path, however, he noticed muscular men with long blonde hair sitting at the base of some of the cedar trees. Crouched in the snow with helmets and swords at their side, they barely moved.

'Er – Taymar,'

'They're foot soldiers,' Taymar cut in. They guard the path to Mrs Peabody's house.

'Why is Mrs Peabody so important?'

Taymar looked over her shoulder. 'She's the only way to the Exiles.'

They came upon the house, a huge lion head's knocker fastened to the shiny black door. Taymar took the knocker in her hand and rapped it three times.

While they were waiting, Benjamin looked around. The cottage was nestled tightly in to the side of the hill leading to the train tracks. Its thatched roof was almost camouflaged by the overgrown shrubs and wild plants on the hill. All over the front garden, little pink and yellow flowers poked through the covering of snow.

'Awright girl, up ya go,' Jeems spoke out of nowhere. Primrose lifted up and flew over the house, brushing the roof with her belly. She looked as though she was going to crash right in to the hill but dove straight down behind the house.

'She's in the back,' Jeems answered Benjamin's puzzled look.

The door swung open and a short, stocky lady that almost swallowed the width of the doorway stood in front of them. With tight grey curls and horn-rimmed glasses, Benjamin mused that she looked like something out of a comic book.

'Well, hello there,' the woman said in a perky voice. 'What a pleasant surprise. Mind you, I had some warning that you may be passing through.' She grinned broadly and winked at Jeems.

'Well, come on in, it's cold outside!' She stepped out of the way as they stomped through the doorway. 'I'm Mrs Peabody,' she said to Benjamin as he came through. 'And you must be Benjamin.'

Benjamin nodded dumbly, unable to take his eyes off her. Her face was covered in thick, bright make-up, her short neck swallowed up by three chins. Her flowered dress matched her bright blue eyeshadow, and her pearl earrings looked like they were stuck out from either side of her head. She bent down to kiss Benjamin on the cheek, leaving a layer of bright red lipstick plastered to the side of his face.

'Come, come and sit down,' she said showing the three in to the main living area. 'Is Primrose alright, Jeems?'

Jeems nodded. 'Flew in ter the back just before ya opened the door. Thanks fer askin'.'

'Good, good,' Mrs Peabody nodded enthusiastically. 'You can never be too sure these days. Do you like hot chocolate, Benjamin?'

'Uh – yes, very much,' he answered.

'That is a boy after my own heart,' she answered. 'Nothing tastes better on a cold day after a race against a few bedruggers than a big mug of hot chocolate.'

They made general conversation while Mrs Peabody set to work melting a huge bar of chocolate with cream in a pot over the fire. Jeems filled Mrs Peabody in on what they had all just been through. She listened intently, her eyes going from all three of them with equal amounts of concern on her face. The conversation soon lost on him, Benjamin scanned the room. The walls and thick beams were covered with framed black and white photos of various people. Pots of bright coloured flowers were on every surface, clashing with the bright red carpet that ran throughout the room. Hutches and shelves were crammed full of china dishes, old photos and other little figurines. An old radio stood on a beautiful upright piano that looked as though it had been well played over the years.

'You sure have a lot of friends,' Benjamin remarked, scanning the photos.

Mrs Peabody smiled, not taking her eyes off the pot. 'Most of them are my brothers and sisters. There were seven of us.'

'Whoa,'

'That's the way things were back then,' Mrs Peabody poured thick steaming chocolate in to four stone mugs. 'Everyone had big families – well, mostly everyone.'

'So were there lots of people around when you were a kid?' Benjamin asked.

Mrs Peabody nodded. 'Early on, yes. Then things changed.' She stopped talking for a moment and handed Benjamin a mug. 'I'm sure you have been told that Meridia is not what it used to be.'

Benjamin nodded and slurped his drink. The smooth chocolate warmed his entire body.

'Well, if you ask me, there's going to be more changes. Some for the worse, but in the end it will work out, I'm sure.'

The steam from Mrs Peabody's cup rose up and settled on her glasses.

'You'll see,' she said reassuringly. 'There is a time for everything, and soon it will be Meridia's time once again.'

Benjamin smiled and sipped his chocolate. He sat down next to Jeems, who was talking to Taymar about someone called Hubrice.

'I'm tellin' ya. He won't like it, not one bit,' Jeems mumbled.

'Now that's enough you two,' Mrs Peabody scolded playfully. 'There'll be no negative thoughts in this house, you should both know better.' Jeems looked down, like a school boy who had just been scolded.

'But speaking of Hubrice,' Mrs Peabody said after moment, 'you two wouldn't care to help me with some dinner, would you?' She looked at Taymar and Jeems.

'That won't be any trouble,' Taymar responded, standing up.

'Right, thank you.' Mrs Peabody continued. 'You know where to find everything? The vegetables in the cellar?' She then looked outside. 'There's not much snow on the ground, so I should think there will be a few rabbits out back. I have these two that we caught earlier,' Mrs Peabody pointed to the kitchen counter. 'But that won't be enough.'

'Urck,' Benjamin sputtered, shuddering from the chill that ran up his spine.

Mrs Peabody laughed. 'Animals are given to us to eat. Don't worry, they get taken care of too. Look at how fat that one is,' she pointed to the larger of the two. 'He's eaten well, and now it's his time to give back.'

Benjamin followed Taymar and Jeems but was called back. 'I'd much prefer if you stayed to help me in the garden, Benjamin,' Mrs Peabody said sweetly from the kitchen. 'If that's alright with you, of course.'

Benjamin looked from the rabbits on the counter to Jeems, who patted him on the back and gave a quick nod. 'She's as sweet as they come, lad. Ya'll be fine. An' we'll be back in no time.' He took a breath and turned back to Mrs Peabody who had a big basket in her hands.

'Care to come outside and help me pick some quips?' She said.

11

The Unwelcome Visitor

'I thought you were going to make me doing something with those rabbits,' Benjamin said as he followed Mrs Peabody outside. The back garden was surprisingly big considering the position of the house. Stretching about 100 yards either way, a vegetable patch ran along the right hand side of the fence, although not much was in it due to the season. A high, ivy-covered fence enclosed the garden on either side, with the hill at the back. Along the back was a flower garden that stretched the entire width, overgrown, but beautiful and inviting. In the middle of the flowers was a stone archway that looked like it led to something. A large tree stood in the left corner, its green leaves and purple buds wrapped in frost.

'What's that dear?' Mrs Peabody was already knee deep in her garden, picking off dead buds.

'I said I thought you were going to make me doing something with those rabbits,' Benjamin repeated. Primrose nuzzled up to him before finding a spot in the garden to lie down.

Mrs Peabody straightened up. 'Oh, no,' she puffed. 'Jeems and Taymar can see to those. We're here to pick quips.'

She led Benjamin to the bottom of the garden towards the tree. 'What's a quip?' He asked.

'A kind of fruit that grows in Meridia. Here you go, just pick them off at the stem.' She put the basket on the ground and set to picking the purple buds off the frosted tree. Benjamin copied her and they were silent for a while, Mrs Peabody humming softly to herself.

'Mrs Peabody, Jeems told me that those bedruggers were watching your house.'

'Hm-mm. They've come and gone over the years, but since you last left Meridia they've been there without fail.'

Benjamin furled his eyebrows. 'Why don't they come after you?'

Mrs Peabody picked a few more quips. 'I just love being in my back garden. You know, when I built this house, the garden was a mess.' She smiled and shook her head. 'It was the worst I had ever seen. There were rocks – big ones that needed to be taken out. Weeds as high as you that needed to be pulled. I had to use an axe on a few of them. But still, bit by bit it took shape and now it's beautiful.'

'You did this all by yourself? It must have taken a long time.'

'I had help along the way,' she answered. 'Gideon came everyday to help me clear out the debris – the stuff that needed to be thrown away. Sometimes it was easy, sometimes it was real sweaty work. But as long as I was willing to work on it, he came.'

'Do you still see him sometimes?'

'Everyday.'

'Every day!' Benjamin exclaimed. 'Really? Has he already been today?'

Mrs Peabody nodded. 'But that's not to say he won't be back. Sometimes he comes when I call him. Sometimes he comes just to hang around. It all depends what state the garden is in.'

'I didn't know Gideon liked gardening,' Benjamin remarked.

'He likes the harvest,' Mrs Peabody replied.

'So I guess that's why the bedruggers leave you alone, then. Because Gideon's always around.'

'That's exactly right young man.'

'It sounds like he really takes care of you,' Benjamin said, staring at a particularly big berry.

'He certainly does,' Mrs Peabody answered.

Benjamin bit his lip, his eyes fixed on the same berry.

'These quips sure are hearty,' Mrs Peabody smiled and shook her head as she spoke. 'To be able to grow in the winter.'

Benjmain made a noise that was barely audible.

She came up to Benjamin with a few buds in her hands. 'You'd never think something so fragile could stand this cold, but look. When it's summer time, the quip grows without these leaves around it.' Mrs Peabody pulled back the purple leaves. A dark purple berry was nestled in the leaves, sweet and juicy. 'But in the winter,' she continued, 'the leaves wrap themselves around the berry to protect it from the cold.'

Benjamin looked at it intently. 'It's like it has a brain.'

'No dear. It's just taken care of. Even though it may look like it's forgotten, covered in frost, it's taken care of. When I look at these quips, Benjamin, I remember that even though I may not feel like it sometimes, somebody out there loves me enough to make sure I'm alright.'

They stood there for a minute, looking at each other. Light snowflakes floated down, settling softly on their shoulders as the sun set. A noise from the house caused them both to turn. Jeems and Taymar emerged with what Benjamin assumed were rabbits and vegetables wrapped in canvas and piled in to three wheel barrels.

'Oh, your timing is perfect!' Mrs Peabody handed Benjamin the basket which was now full of quips. 'Okay, off you go. We'll see you soon,'

'Where are we going?' Benjamin asked Jeems as he balanced the basket on top of one of the wheel barrels and fell in line behind him.

'Ter the Exiles.'

'Oh,' Benjamin answered.

'They are the lost people,' Taymar chipped in.

'Okay,' he answered, stumbling along after them through the stone arch that was built in to the hill at the back of the garden. He looked back and waved to Primrose, who was sulking about the fact that she was too big to go through the opening.

They walked for a few minutes in silence.

'So, er, where are we going again?

Jeems stopped, sighed deeply and turned around to face Benjamin.

'Ya know, ya've bin so much a part of me life fer the past 12 years, I sometimes ferget ya know nuthin'.'

Benjamin blushed in the darkness. 'Sorry.'

'Ya know how Taymar was sayin' 'bout there bein' lots o' people in Meridia at one time?'

'Yeah.'

'An' how it's gotten where no'uns really around.'

Benjamin nodded.

'Well, there's a group o' people that escaped all the raids by the bedruggers and the like.'

'Really? Maybe my parents –'

Jeems raised his hand. 'Now don't go thinkin' stuff up.'

Benjamin's shoulders dropped and he looked at his feet.

'I'm sorry, mate,' Jeems said softly. 'There's no chance o' that, so there isn't.'

'Right,' Benjamin recovered. 'So you were saying?'

'Oh – right,' Jeems cleared his throat. 'So there's bin a group o' people who 'scaped, an' with

Gideon's help, they've bin waitin' down here 'til the time comes when they can live freely in Meridia again.'

'Okay?'

Jeems turned and started walking again. Taymar had gone ahead of them and was out of sight.

'Most 'o them are friendly enough, so they are,' Jeems continued. 'But there's a few ya gotta watch.'

'Right.'

'Oh, an' don't 'spect a warm welcome from ol' Hubrice Lack. He won't like ya bein' here.'

'Hubrice?'

Before Jeems could answer they came upon a large open room. Taymar's cart was beside her and she was talking to a very grumpy looking man.

'-he needs protection from Magh and her legions,' Taymar's voice dropped to a whisper as Benjamin approached.

Jeems led them in to the large round room. To the left were four archways attached to tunnels. Jeems ushered Benjamin around one of the three long tables to where a number of women were busy unpacking Taymar's cart.

'Awright, Patience?' Jeems asked a small woman with long brown hair. Without stopping, she glanced up at him and gave a quick nod.

Jeems looked over his shoulder to where Hubrice and Taymar were in a heated but whispered discussion. 'Hubrice not happy?'

Patience looked briefly towards Benjamin and shook her head. 'He's still hurting.' She came towards Benjamin. 'I'll take that,' she said, motioning towards the cart he carried in.

'Oh – sorry. Here you go.' She smiled weakly and took it from Benjamin, took the basket of quips off the top and went towards the huge wood stove where other women were separating the food and wood. Once the food was divided evenly in to three piles, two of the carts were taken down separate tunnels by other women, while Patience stayed at the stove with the third.

'There's two more rooms like this one further down them tunnels,' Jeems explained.

'Hm,' Benjamin said numbly. His gaze was fixed on the man that Taymar was talking to. As tall as Taymar was, the grumpy looking man was very stocky. She had just motioned for them both to sit down, and the man was looking slightly less grumpy when Jeems tugged Benjamin's elbow.

'Let's go,' he muttered to Benjamin.

'Er-' Benjamin didn't move his feet.

'Ya'll have ter get it o'er with sooner or later,' Jeems said quietly in his ear. 'There's no sayin' how long we'll be here fer, but it'll be a while before them bedruggers stop lookin' fer ya day an' night. So makin' yer peace with Hubrice now'll make it easier on every'un, so it will. Believe me.'

'But I haven't done anything wrong, have I?'

'Na, but, well, it ain't as easy as that,' Jeems sighed impatiently. 'Just c'mon. Me an' Taymar won't let him bully ya.'

They approached the long table where Taymar and Hubrice were sat. Along the far end two young men were playing some kind of game with dice. Along the other table children were drawing; their fathers drinking from tin cups and talking quietly, looking over from time to time. Down from them was a boy slightly older than Benjamin, sitting with an elderly woman. The boy looked quite interested in what was going on, and Benjamin wished he would vanish.

As they sat down, Hubrice straightened up.

'Awright Hubrice,' Jeems nodded. 'This 'ere's-'

'Oh, you don't have to bother with introductions,' Hubrice grumbled. 'I know who he is.' Hubrice's eyes burned holes in to Benjamin. His long brown hair was streaked with grey; coarse and bushy that matched his scruffy whiskers. His ears were lost in his thick neck, and his shoulders spanned the width of the table. Even though he was sitting down, he was still up to Benjamin's chin.

'You,' he pointed a thick finger at Benjamin, revealing a layer of dirt under his fingernails. 'You're the one. Gideon's favourite.'

'Now that's not necessary, mate,' Jeems said in a low voice. By now everyone in the room was looking at the scene unfolding. The small group of women that had been busying themselves by the wood stove earlier had slowed or stopped what they were doing. Only Patience and another woman kept working.

'No, you're probably right,' Hubrice continued. Benjamin felt his muscles relax. 'But there's lots of things in this world that aren't necessary now, aren't there?'

Hubrice raised his eyebrows and looked directly at Benjamin. 'Aren't there?'

Benjamin swallowed hard. 'I suppose,' he said quietly.

Hubrice looked at him intently. He nodded slowly. 'I'm glad I've had the chance to meet you. You know, Benjamin, you remind me of someone.'

'Hubrice, we spoke of this,' Taymar leaned over the table and looked Hubrice right in the face. 'There is nothing to be gained.'

'There's nothing to be gained anyways,' Hubrice responded dismissively, his eyes still locked on Benjamin.

The room was quiet, except for the sound of Patience and a young girl getting pots and pans down off the shelves that had been built in to the wall to the right of the woodstove. Another little girl that looked just like the other one was carefully placing tin plates down on the far table.

'Are you not interested in who you remind me of?' Hubrice asked Benjamin, a thin frown on his face.

Benjamin didn't answer.

'Or is it *whom* where you come from?' Hubrice chuckled. 'Of course, that's wrong isn't it? Because you're from Meridia.' Hubrice hunched over again. 'Maybe it's best not to say where you *come from*, but rather *where you were hidden.* Hidden so you, and only you could be saved.'

'Gideon'll not be happy,' Jeems said quietly to Hubrice.

Hubrice broke his gaze from Benjamin to look at Jeems. 'Gideon? Gideon? Gideon who? I haven't seen Gideon for such a long time I think I've forgotten what he looks like.' Hubrice stood up to address the rest of his captive audience. 'Has anybody here seen or heard from Gideon?'

Then silent stares for the better part of a few minutes. Everyone was looking at Hubrice. As he slowly walked down the length of the table, Taymar stood up, taking position behind Benjamin.

The little girl who had the plates in her hands came up to Hubrice. 'I talked to Gideon daddy. He said that he's always willing to talk to people who want to listen to him.'

Hubrice looked down at his daughter. He stroked her brown hair and tenderly, more tenderly than Benjamin thought possible, touched her cheek.

'Well,' he choked. 'Looks like he's fooled another member of my family.' He turned the little girl back to the arms of Patience, who received her with tears in her eyes. 'Fools,' Hubrice muttered as he wove in and out of the tables. 'That is what he takes us for.'

'Now see 'ere,' Jeems started, but Taymar held his arm.

'It is not for us to defend,' she said to him quietly.

'You don't agree?' Hubrice raised his eyebrows and looked at Jeems. 'Then tell me, *mate*, how are we supposed to feel now. Now that there is apparently a spy among us.'

A murmur went through the large crowd that had gathered. People filed in from the tunnels to where they were all standing. Hubrice came and stood right beside the three of them and Benjamin secretly wished Primrose was here to breathe on this overgrown hot air balloon.

'It is true, my friends, we have a spy among us.' Hubrice addressed the growing crowd. 'There is a constant presence of bedruggers, tatty's, or even the odd Raptor outside of these walls. Always keeping watch. Our only shield an old woman.'

'Ya've bin givin' a lot more pertection than that Hubrice, an' ya know it,' Jeems growled. Benjamin saw Jeems clench his hands. His guts did the same.

'Then how, may we ask, has Magh come to know that we are down here?' Hubrice looked around at everyone. 'Gideon is the one who saw fit to bring us together, and now it appears as though we have a traitor amongst us. He takes us for fools. We are in a mess and he has left us here to rot.' A general air of agreement floated over the crowd. Benjamin noticed only a few who didn't nod, one being the boy who continued to sit at the table with the old woman.

'The only fool here is you, my friend,' Taymar advanced on Hubrice. 'The mess you are in-'

'Gideon is the reason we're in this mess!' Hubrice shouted. His eyes flashed, and his little girl whimpered, hiding her face in Patience's apron.

'*You* are the reason you're in this mess,' Taymar retorted. Her voice was firm, her words hung in the air. The murmurs quieted again and everyone looked on. Fathers had sent their children down in to the tunnels and were starting to wager who would win the argument.

Taymar continued. 'You and you alone. And you know that. Gideon tried to keep you from making foolish decisions but you wouldn't listen. All you saw was glory – glory for your family and glory for yourself. You took your eyes off the truth and paid attention to lies. So now you're here. Here for

150

protection not only from Magh, but from yourselves.' Taymar's voice tailed off. She pushed passed Hubrice and down one of the tunnels.

'My family deserves the glory!' Hubrice shouted after her. 'We are the only ones left – direct descendant from Horatio himself.' Hubrice turned back to look at Benjamin. 'Did you hear me? My family! Not some troublemaker from a long line of failures.'

The last comment caused a blast of heat across Benjamin's face. He turned away from the crowd, searching for an empty space near the walls. He noticed Hubrice was close to tears, but that didn't matter to him now.

'Hubrice, ya went too far,' Jeems said in a strained voice. The air became heavy and no one spoke. Then a scratching sound from one of the tunnels.

Scuffling out of the side tunnel, a short man with long, wispy hair came towards Hubrice. Once level with him, he put his wrinkled hand on the large man's back.

'Noone doubts the dignity of your lineage,' my friend.

Hubrice nodded curtly, looking straight ahead. Benjamin kept his eyes on a spot on the wall.

151

The old man made his way over to where Benjamin and Jeems were standing. He looked brittle, like a dry twig that could snap with little force. The only thing that cut through Benjamin's uneasiness was the warm smile on the man's face, deepening the wrinkles around his mouth and eyes.

'It is a pleasure to meet you,' the man croaked as he held out his hand to Benjamin.

'This 'ere's Jericho Twist,' Jeems introduced the two.

'Hi,' Benjamin replied uneasily. He took Jericho's hand gently.

Everyone that had been watching before went back to their business. A few of Hubrice's friends and family rallied around him, coaxing him to sit down to a frosty mug of foamy drink. Some of the crowd dispersed back through the tunnels where they came, while others milled about talking and helping prepare the room for dinner.

Jericho looked at Benjamin with steely blue eyes. 'I must say, we have been waiting for you for a very long time,' Jericho's smile never left his transparent looking face. 'But of course, timing is everything, and nothing that we here have any control over. But enough of that. You must be very tired. I would be most honoured to host you in my hovel for the length of your stay.'

Benjamin looked at Jeems. 'Er – uh,'

'No need, thanks, Jericho,' Jeems held out his hand and took a side step closer to Benjamin. 'Taymar's sortin' us out. She'll have her own down the back an' Benjermin an' me'll share one, so we will.' Jeems motioned with his lips in the direction that Taymar had stormed down the tunnel.

Jericho raised his eyebrows and hesitated for a moment. 'Oh,' he said, finally making eye contact with Jeems. 'I assumed you and your .... *friend* would be on your way once you were sure of the boy's safety.'

Jeems chuckled softly and shook his head. 'No, we're here fer a while. We stay with Benjermin from 'ere on in, so we do,' Jeems gave Benjamin a quick wink, who felt his body relax slightly.

Jericho didn't speak for a few moments, but just looked from Jeems to Benjamin. 'Of course, I understand,' he said after a few awkward moments. 'You must have orders. Well, I do have things I must attend to.' He bowed his head and walked away.

Jeems shook his head playfully. 'Good ol' Jericho,' he said fondly. 'Always thinkin' 'bout every'un else but himself.'

'Really?' Benjamin asked, bewildered. 'He kind of gives me the creeps.'

'Jericho?' Jeems looked astounded. 'He's harmless!' 'Might look a little rough 'round the edges, but would give ya the shirt off his back, so he would.'

'If you say so,' Benjamin murmured and raised his eyebrows.

As everyone was gathering around for dinner, Jeems and Benjamin decided to find Taymar. They met her coming back up the tunnel she had gone down earlier. She looked much calmer than before, and gave them a big smile when she approached.

'You were really angry,' Benjamin said reproachfully. But to his pleasant surprise, Taymar's immediate response was a kind, gentle nod.

'I'm sorry about that, little warrior,' she replied. They walked along a bit more. 'I do not understand how people can sometimes be so close-minded. Surely people should be thankful for what they have rather than what they do not have, or above all, what they have lost.'

After thinking about what Taymar said, Benjamin figured she was right. He had never really had anything to speak of. It had only been since he started coming to Meridia that he really felt like he could do anything. Most days, he couldn't even manage to get to school on time because of being pushed around by Huxley and his gang. Even now there were times that he felt down about things. He ashamedly recalled a few times since being in Meridia this time that he found himself wishing he was back at Mr and Mrs Winks' home. He shot a sideways glance to Taymar, suspicious that she could read his mind.

The three entered the main hall where a large crowd had gathered for dinner. Men, women and children were sat at the long tables, steaming food piled on their plates. They joined the end of the queue for food.

'Hey Taymar, looks like we came at the right time,' Jeems motioned over to where Hubrice was sitting, finishing off a plate of quip pie. He looked deep in conversation with a few other men, one who looked a lot like him.

'That's his brother there,' Jeems whispered. 'He's got a big family. Loads of brothers an' sisters.'

'Are they all here?'

Jeems shook his head slowly. 'Na. Some are. One or two have died, and the next oldest one, well, he's on the other side, so he is. So Hubrice is now looked on as the leader of the family, if ya like.'

'So, do you mean that Hubrice's brother is like those two guys we saw in the trees?' Benjamin watched Hubrice eating the rest of his pie slowly, taking in the conversation around him. Their eyes met and Benjamin quickly looked away.

'Summat like that, only a bit higher up,' Jeems answered. He filled his bowl with some rabbit stew. 'That's how Hubrice got that scar over his eye.' Benjamin turned back to Hubrice and noticed the burn scar running down over his right eye.

'What happened?'

'Well,' Jeems said through a mouthful of bread. He handed Benjamin a bowl of stew and followed Taymar to the nearest table. 'Him and his older brother, Firmitas got in ter a right ding dong, so they did. Firmitas thought the only way ter go was with Magh, but Hubrice didn't see things that way.'

Benjamin nodded attentively. Taymar listened closely, dunking her bread in her bowl.

'Hubrice tried ter stop Firmitas from goin' o'er ter the other side, so he did. He was convinced, an' still is, that it was their family that was ter stop Magh once an' fer all. When Firmitas tried ter convince Hubrice otherwise they got in ter it, but good.'

'Looks like it,' Benjamin replied.

Jeems nodded. 'They was in the middle o' the blacksmith shop. That shop had been in the family fer o'er hundred years.'

'And?'

'When they got fightin', didn't Firimitas just take a hot poker ter Hubrice. That's how he got the scar. Hubrice went mad. They got thrashin' stuff about and before ya knew it the place was on fire.'

None of them spoke for a few minutes. Benjamin kept stealing glances over to Hubrice. He had cheered up some and was talking to what Benjamin assumed was his sister, as she looked so much like him.

'If Hubrice believed then that Gideon was right, how come he's so against him now?' Benjamin dipped his bread in his stew and licked it cautiously.

Taymar and Jeems looked at each other. 'Hubrice wants glory, little warrior, not the truth.' Taymar finished her dinner and with one reproachful look over to Hubrice, left the table to speak to a group of people who dressed as odd as she did.

'She's just sore, is all,' Jeems explained. 'She can't understand that sometimes people have doubt.'

'Well, she must feel the same way sometimes,' Benjamin replied.

'Not Taymar,' Jeems responded. 'She's on a different level than you or me.'

'You can say that again,' Benjamin said through a mouthful of quip pie. 'These quips are pretty tasty,' he commented.

Just then Jericho Twist walked by and sat at the next table where he received a very warm welcome.

'People 'ere really rate Jericho, so they do,' Jeems said watching the little man. Benjamin joined in for a moment, thinking that he will probably need a few friends down in these tunnels. He noticed how Jericho was quite animated when he spoke, but not loud and boisterous like Hubrice.

'Funny,' Jeems continued. 'Him bein' a latecomer an' all, how well folk took ter him.'

'I don't understand, Jeems.'

'Jericho was the last one ter come ter this place. An' then he was here fer a while and then just disappeared fer a few weeks. When he came back it was clear ter every'un that he must've left in some kind o' daze o' grief, as he had lost his wife not long before he came.'

Benjamin nodded.

'Most people look ter Hubrice ter say things like it is, no matter how badly he gets it wrong sometimes. But every'un seems ter find comfort in Jericho every now an' again. It's just the way he is.'

People slowly filed out of the main room, but Benjamin decided to hang back and help clear up. After Hubrice's outburst, he didn't want people to think he was someone special, so he offered to get stuck in.

Jeems gave him a pat on the back and joined Taymar in a card game with a group at the far side of the room. Benjamin had just started drying the dishes when the boy he had seen earlier came up beside him.

'Don't worry about Hubrice, he's got a lot of hot air,' the boy said, flicking his messy hair out of his eyes. He was slightly taller than Benjamin with hair down to his shoulders. He had a number of freckles on his face and light brown eyes to match his hair. Although most of the people down here looked generally unkempt, he seemed to be more ragged than most with his dirty oversized shirt that fell off his shoulder on one side. It was tied in at the waist by an old leather belt that matched his worn out leather boots and cut-off trousers.

'They keep it really warm down here,' the boy said, looking at his dirty bare legs. 'My name's Will. Will Bottlemaker.'

'Benjamin.' He continued drying and stacking plates.

Will picked up a towel. 'Some of us have been talking, and we never thought we'd ever see you.'

'Why?'

'Well, it's obvious, isn't it? There's loads of talk that we have a traitor in the place, so we're all just waiting for the Raptors to come and raid us. Having you hidden here is like offering candy to a baby.'

'Raptors can't get in here,' Benjamin shook his head. 'Not with Mrs Peabody up there. And on top of that she's got a load of foot soldiers in her front garden.' He kept drying. 'And don't forget Primrose, she's up there as well.'

'Well, some think that Mrs Peabody won't be able to hold them off forever,' Will replied. 'And as far as the foot soldiers go, they can only do what Gideon tells them to do. And Primrose?' Will raised one eyebrow and smirked. 'I heard that she's afraid of her own shadow.'

Benjamin laughed. 'You're right about Primrose, but I'm not sure about everything else.'

'I'm not saying I believe that stuff,' Will raised his hands and backed up, causing a high pile of plates to sway slightly. 'I'm just telling you some of the talk.

Me and my grandmother believe what Gideon's been telling us all along.'

'What's that?'

'As if you don't know,' Will scoffed.

Embarrassed, and wanting to change the subject, Benjamin glanced over to Hubrice. 'What's his problem anyways?'

'He gets full of himself sometimes. The whole family used to be really popular, but ever since his son died –'

'What?' Benjamin said it louder than even he was expecting, catching the attention of a few people.

'Keep your voice down,' Will looked at him sternly.

'Anyways, yeah,' Will nodded. 'It was horrible. Although I was too young to remember it. His name was Jasper. He died when he was a few months old.'

Benjamin dried the same plate four times, never taking his eyes off Will.

'Wasn't just him, neither. Loads of baby boys died at the same time.'

Will could only nod at Benjamin's look of horror. 'That's how this place filled up so quick. After that, Magh really let loose.'

161

'Magh?' Benjamin's voice echoed across half the room, this time causing Jeems and Taymar to take notice. Will turned away and purposely dropped a stack of plates. Under the accusing eyes of the kitchen ladies, they both bent down to pick them up,.

'Boy you're loud,' Will whispered when they were down on their knees. 'We can't talk about this here. I'll meet you outside of your hovel once Jeems is asleep.'

'Right. I assume a hovel is a bedroom?'

'You catch on quick.'

12

Stories of an Old Woman

'Jeems, is everything ok?' Benjamin tried to hide his impatience as Jeems squirmed in his bed.

'It's this,' Jeems grunted and shifted uncomfortably on the squeaky bed. 'This darn pillow. I hate feather pillows, they scratch me face, so they do.' He propped himself up on his elbow and punched his pillow a few times. 'And – they- never-stay-puffed-up,' he added, striking it with every word.

'You can have mine,' Benjamin offered. Jeems stopped what he was doing.

'Are ya sayin' yers in't got feathers in it?' Benjamin scrunched his pillow. 'I think it does, but, I thought if you needed it, you could have mine as well.'

'What, like, take yers as well, ya mean?' Jeems asked suspiciously.

'Sure,' Benjamin shrugged his shoulders.

Jeems looked at Benjamin, and for a moment he thought Jeems would know something was up.

'Don't be daft, ya need yer own pillow,' Jeems said finally. 'This place is as good a hideout as any

Gideon's dreamed up, but one thing it don't have, and that's good pillows. Yer gonna need yers, ya better keep it.'

Jeems turned over, his back to Benjamin. After wrestling a moment longer, he let out an exasperated sigh and settled down. Minutes later he was snoring.

Checking that Jeems was truly asleep, Benjamin crept out of the hovel and waited in the long corridor for Will.

Thoughts filled his head as he waited in the dark. Why did Hubrice say that he came from a long line of failures? From what Gideon had told him, his parents were anything but losers. His thoughts went back to Hubrice's son Jasper. If Jasper died twelve years ago, that would make them the same age. So how come Jasper died if he was sent to Hadley Priest? Benjamin sighed deeply and looked up to the low ceiling. It suddenly occurred to him Christmas had come and gone and he hadn't even thought about it. He closed his eyes and imagined what it would have been like at Mr and Mrs Wink's house. He could almost smell the turkey and roast potatoes.

'Psst!' Benjamin's eyes shot open, his heart in his throat.

'Benjamin?'

'Is that you, Will?' He squinted through the darkness, barely able to see Will standing next to Taymar's hovel.

Will motioned for Benjamin to follow him, and they both set off down the tunnel, turning right down a small side tunnel and in to a small hovel.

Will pulled the curtain across the entrance and lit the candles that sat on his small bedside table.

'Is this your hovel, or room, or whatever?' Benjamin asked, looking around. It was like Benjamin's, but smaller as it was built for one person rather than two. The dirt floor was well trampled, with a few pictures on the rough dirt walls.

'Yep,' said Will as he crawled under his bed. 'It's really small and sometimes it gets to me,' he called out from under the bed. 'But it's better than going over to the other side.'

'Do you think you would?'

'It's either that or die up there,' Will replied, coming out. It didn't seem to bother him that he was covered in dirt. In his hand he held a package wrapped in brown paper, a string loosely tied around it, outlining the rectangle shape.

Benjamin looked at the package with interest as Will tossed it on his bed, next to where he sat.

'What were we talking about at dinner?'

'Er – Hubrice?' Benjamin sat next to Will, the package between them. Will nodded and pulled his legs up to his chest.

'Well, like I said, a whole load of baby boys died during that time,' his voice dropped to a whisper.

'I don't get it,' Benjamin shook his head.

Will shrugged his shoulders. 'From what I know, it was like an announcement was made about finding a leader for the Potens group.'

Benjamin raised his eyebrows.

'Like government groups,' Will flicked his hands in the air as he talked.

'Oh right, like the Prime Minister and stuff,' Benjamin nodded. 'Gideon told me that Meridia used to have a pretty good government.'

'For a while they did,' Will continued. Then loads of people started to follow this group called the Potens. And they eventually got voted in. So anyways, the Potens made this announcement about an oracle that was said long ago, and how it was time to figure out who the leader was going to be to bring the party in to the *next generation*.' He rolled his eyes.

Benjamin sat back against the wall.

'They convinced most folk that the oracle said the next leader was still a baby, but it was important that they knew who it was right away so the child could grow up to learn his destiny.' Will rolled his eyes again. 'They said loads of rubbish like, the kid's family would go down in history for leading Meridia in to glory, blah, blah, blah.'

'I'm confused, Will.'

Will shook his head. 'Don't be. Some of this stuff isn't important. The point is that they told everyone who had a baby boy to put this special oil on their kids' heads before bed on this one particular night. The baby who was meant to be leader would have gold dust on their head the next morning.'

'What!' Benjamin gawked.

'Shhh!' Will hissed and turned to the curtain. After a few moments he continued. 'I know, it's mad, but, it just goes to show you how stupid people can be sometimes.'

'So let me guess, Hubrice was the only one that believed this tosh.' Benjamin said.

'Na-uh,' Will shook his head. Benjamin's mouth dropped open. 'There were loads of parents who jumped at the chance of their kid being the next leader. They opened a few collection places throughout

167

Meridia for this special oil. People travelled for days. And as the Potens were giving it out for free, everyone could get it.'

Benjamin shook his head from side to side. 'I can't believe people could be so stupid.'

'Well, it's not that far-fetched here, really,' Will said defensively. 'Things happen in Meridia that you've never seen before.'

'True.'

'Exactly. And strictly speaking, gold dust in Meridia is not uncommon. It doesn't happen every day,' Will emphasised, noticing Benjamin's expression. 'But in the old days when sentaphs were around more, well, anyways, we're off topic and you can't stay much longer.'

'Right, okay, so you were saying.'

Will sighed deeply. 'Okay, so loads of people got this oil and then on a specific day – I don't really know the date or whatever, but they were supposed to rub the oil on at night and the kid with the gold dust on his head was the next leader of the Potens group.'

'And if not?'

'Well, if not, then nothing. But,'

'They all died,' Benjamin finished softly.

Will nodded. 'Every last one of them. Well, the Potens claimed that they found the one they were looking for, but nobody has ever seen him.'

'But Will, that's like really bad. Didn't the Potens get blamed for all those deaths?'

'Mostly,' Will agreed. 'And that's when it all kicked off.' 'The Potens tried to say it was their way of weeding out the bad ones. Some of the diehards, like Hubrice stormed the homes of where top Potens officials lived. And that's when Magh got busy.'

'What about Howl?'

Will shook his head and sighed. '*He* never comes out himself, does he? He keeps himself holed away like some chicken. But he sent Magh who sent out Raptors and Tatty's. They started to beat people and burn their homes, all in the name of public order. The Potens found a way to blame the whole thing on Gideon and the sentaphs that were around. So some people turned against them.'

'So what did Gideon do?'

'Nothing publicly,' Will replied. 'Gideon's a more personal bloke. He knew the ones who still believed him, and that's how we ended up here. The ones who never signed up to the Potens ended up being hidden away until, well, until you would come.'

There was silence for quite some time, and Benjamin was sure Will could hear his mind whirring with everything.

'Do you get it?' Will finally asked.

'Kind of,' Benjamin said slowly. 'There's lots of gaps.'

'Well, yeah, there would be. I was only two years old when this all kicked off. My grandmother told me everything I know.'

'Who's she?'

'She's my grandmother!' Will answered and shook his head. 'Sheesh. Her and I came here about ten years ago, after the Raptors got my parents.'

'Sorry.'

Will shrugged. 'Thanks. It got easier over time. They died for something good. And they died saving me and my grandmother, so I'm quite proud of them.'

'I never really thought if it that way.'

'What way?'

'Being proud rather than angry,' Benjamin sighed deeply. 'I always just felt so cheated that I never knew my parents. I never really thought about feeling anything other than sad and lonely.'

'It was different for you, though. You got whisked away. At least I got to live here with my grandmother who told me the truth. You've always been kept in the dark.'

'Yeah.'

'My grandmother thinks the whole thing was a setup to find you,' Will continued. He had stood up and was rummaging through an old box in the corner of his hovel.

'Er-'

'The thing about Jasper,' Will repeated. 'Keep up, would ya,' he said jokingly as he poked his head out of the box. He flashed Benjamin a smile. 'She reckons that they only knew a bit of what the oracle was, not all of it, and they thought by killing all of the boys born around the same time they would make sure that the oracle was never raised. But what they didn't count on was that your parents would never follow the Potens.'

'Your grandmother sure knew a lot.'

'Ah, I can't find it,' Will commented and then came back to the bed and sat down. 'My grandmother knew your parents.'

'Really!' Benjamin's face lit up. 'Can I go talk to her?'

Will stopped Benjamin before he made it through the curtain to the corridor.

'No. Not now, anyways. And besides, Ben, can I call you Ben?'

Benjamin nodded.

'You'll have to lay low down here.'

'I can't be any lower.'

Will managed a sarcastic smirk. 'What I'm trying to say is, that some people are starting to doubt why they're here. Some are starting to wonder if they would be better off up above,' Will pointed to the ceiling. 'Loads are happy to sit tight until the time comes for them to go up again. We all know that it's a war going on and most of us are ready to fight. But some are getting restless.'

'But I'm here now.'

'Yeah, but from what my grandmother says, you've got a long road ahead of you, and that's what makes people think.'

'Think what?'

'...well, that you'll never be able to do it and they'll be stuck down here forever.'

'What makes them think that?' Benjamin shot back, his eyebrows furled.

'Oh, I don't know,' Will mocked. 'Let's see, maybe your age, and your size. Some of the talk I picked up was that they were expecting someone a bit bigger, you see. Someone older.'

'But they must have known it was going to be a child?'

Will nodded. 'Yeah, in general people knew that, but I guess they were expecting an older kid, is all.'

Benjamin thought back to the oracle he raised, and how it talked about him being unremarkable. 'And when I came along they probably thought it was all a lost cause.'

'I don't think that way.'

The two boys shared a smile. Just then they both heard feet scuffling outside. In one fluid motion Will grabbed Benjamin and stuffed him under his bed, while he threw himself under his covers. They both lay perfectly still while the scuffling noise approached Will's hovel. With an enormous blow Will managed to extinguish all three candles before the footsteps reached the entrance. Benjamin dared to breathe, although he didn't really understand what the big deal was. The footsteps eventually scuffled away after lingering for a few minutes. When Will was sure the coast was clear, he slowly got off is bed and helped Benjamin up.

'Will, what was that all about? What are we doing wrong?'

'A curfew was put in place when Hubrice and them suspected there was a traitor down here,' he explained. 'Thanks to Hubrice, anyone caught up after curfew could stand trial for conspiracy.'

'But we're just kids,' Benjamin scoffed.

'It don't matter to Hubrice,' Will answered. 'And you saw him earlier. He would do anything to get something on you. Anyways, here,' Will pushed the package he found earlier in to Benjamin's hand.

'What's this?'

'A picture of your parents and you, before you got sent away,' Will whispered and put his hands in his pockets. 'Your mother gave it to my mother just before, well, anyways. It's funny, you know. I don't remember much of my mother, but I remember looking at that picture when I was little.' He shook his head. 'I don't know what made your mum give that away. She must've known –' Will's voice trailed off. When Benjamin looked up, his eyes were filled with tears.

'Thanks,' Benjamin said hoarsely.

Will nodded, sniffed and swallowed hard. 'They're good to have, pictures. I've got a few and they help sometimes.'

The two orphans stood looking at the package Benjamin was holding. 'Well, I should get going,' Benjamin found his voice.

'Yeah, I'll take you back.' Benjamin put the package in his coat and the two of them crept back down the tunnel, being extra quiet, slightly anxious that someone would catch them. When they had come up to Benjamin's hovel, Jeems was snoring so loudly he was drowning out everything else, so they said goodnight with relief and Benjamin crept in to bed.

Once in bed, he used the dim light of the dying fire to look at the treasure inside the package. His fingers shook as he gingerly unwrapped the paper. In it was a framed photo of his parents holding him when he was a baby. He was amazed at how much he looked like his mother. He studied it for what seemed like hours, until his eyes stung. Rubbing them, he tucked the photo under his pillow and was instantly asleep.

Benjamin dreamed he was walking down the tunnel towards the Exiles, running after two large snakes. When he got to the main room, the two snakes twisted around each other to form a thick rope. They slithered together between many feet, striking at ankles and heels of different people. ...Benjamin tried to speak but couldn't. He tried to warn everyone but no one seemed to notice. He followed them until they struck Jeems' ankle.   ... Jeems was laughing with others and didn't seem to notice. Benjamin turned around and saw Jericho standing alone, watching.

13

Hubrice's Secret

Over the next few weeks Benjamin had the dream about the snakes over and over. He tried to occupy himself by spending a lot of time with Will and some times Jericho, especially when Jeems and Taymar would go up to Mrs Peabody's house. Although Jeems just normally went up to see Primrose, Taymar would be gone for longer periods.

'Jeems, is Taymar coming back?' Benjamin asked one day at breakfast. 'She's been gone for ages.'

Jeems slurped his cereal. ''Bout three days now?' He considered his answer. 'Should be back soon.'

'Where does she go?'

'Can't really say,' Jeems shrugged his shoulders. ''Cause I don't really know meself, so I don't. Gideon's got most o' the sentaphs workin' overtime lately, so he does. She'll be back before we go.'

Benjamin nodded and nibbled on a piece of toast. 'When are we leaving?'

'I reckon things've quieted down some up there, so maybe a few days.'

'Where to this time?'

'Goin' up north,' Jeems answered briskly. 'But Gideon'll be by soon an' we'll talk 'bout it more then.'

Benjamin was pleasantly surprised that Gideon was going to come and see the Exiles. Just as Will had said, many of them had grown restless, and Benjamin couldn't help but notice that some of them whispered behind his back as he walked passed. It made him feel awkward most of the time, and so he took Will's advice and laid as low as he could.

Almost every night the boys would meet at Will's hovel. Most of the time Will would tell Benjamin stories his grandmother told him about life in Meridia before they were sent underground. Benjamin never had much to share, because his life outside of Meridia was so boring. All the same, Will seemed quite interested in Marcus and Riley and everything that happened at Hadley Priest, so he told story after story about the pranks they used to pull on Hester, and Riley's fear of bugs.

'Jeems said that Gideon has the sentaphs working overtime,' Benjamin said to Will one night.

'That makes sense,' Will replied. 'My grandmother reckons that Magh is on the move but proper. That's why you've been down here so long – they must be scouring the whole of Meridia for you.'

'Yeah, I'm famous,' Benjamin remarked sarcastically. 'I always wanted to be popular, but not this way.'

Will chuckled. 'If the sentaphs are working, then Gideon's probably got all the footsoldiers and guardians working as well.'

'Guardians? You mean there's more?' Benjamin asked and flopped down on Will's bed. 'I'm never going to get this place.'

'I've lived here all my life and I still don't get it,' Will said. 'Look here,' he said and drew on the ground with a stick. 'It's kind of like an army, see. You know how in an army there's like generals and commanders and different battalions?'

Benjamin nodded.

'Well, it's the same with the sentaphs. My grandmother said that they have three levels,' Will drew three lines above one another with spaces in between them. 'The lowest one is called Sentaph Ground. That's got your guardians and foot soldiers.'

'I've seen foot soldiers crouched in the bushes in front of Mrs Peabody's house,' Benjamin remarked.

'No doubt they're around,' Will agreed. 'Guardians are sentaphs that used to mix in with folk. You never know who is and isn't a guardian, so you have to be careful.'

Benjamin gave Will a puzzled look.

'Well, I wouldn't want to be mean to a guardian, would you?'

Benjamin thought back to everything he had seen Taymar do since he had met her. 'No, I guess not.'

'Right. Then the second level has got Watchers, Seat Command and Keepers,' Will continued.

'What do they do?'

'I'm not really sure,' Will said and shook his head a little. 'But I don't think we're meant to see them. Mind you, with things going the way they are, I wouldn't be surprised if there's a few up there right now. But anyways, they're like more advanced than the ones in the Sentaph Ground.' Will paused with his stick over the top level. 'That's all I know. My grandmother must have told me the rest at one point, but I guess I just didn't see the need to know at the time.'

'It seems strange how Gideon has an army and Magh is still on the loose,' Benjamin sat on the floor and examined the chart Will had started to construct.

'Oh they have their own army,' Will stated.

'No way.'

'Yeah way,' Will got down on his knees and shook his head. He started drawing lines. 'They have bedruggers on their bottom level.'

'I've seen them.'

Will nodded. 'And then they have Tatty's. You know what they are?'

'Yeah.'

'Good. And then Raptors. But the Raptors are split into three other groups called Legions. Each legion is responsible for certain bad things that happen. Like one certain legion will be responsible for pain and suffering, while another one will be responsible for sickness, another for lies, you know what I mean.'

'Yeah, I think so,' mumbled Benjamin who continued to study what was now quite a complicated chart on the floor. 'And Magh's their leader.'

'She's the deputy,' Will corrected him. 'My grandmother told me that the leader is Howl, but you'll never see him. He thinks he's too good to do anything himself. That's why he created Magh, so she and his henchmen could do everything for him. That, and, I don't think he has much of a body.'

'You're kinda creeping me out,' Benjamin said slowly.

'Well, that's what my grandmother said. I'm not quite sure what she meant, though. She kind of keeps that stuff to herself. She thinks if I know too much about the legions I'll go and join them or something. As if,' Will scoffed and started to rub out the chart with his foot.

'Jeems says we'll be leaving soon.' Will faltered slightly at Benjamin's comment.

'I suppose it had to be soon,' Will answered.

Both boys sat in silence. 'Maybe you could come with me,' Benjamin offered.

Will laughed quietly. 'I'd love to, but my grandmother would never let me. Besides, this is your thing. And you've already got plenty of company.'

'I suppose. Jericho's been hinting about coming.'

'You're joking!' Will struggled to keep his voice down.

Benjamin nodded. 'Yeah, and the funny thing is, Jericho doesn't think I know what he's playing at.'

'Now that's interesting,' Will said thoughtfully. 'Have you told Jeems?'

'I mentioned it,' Benjamin answered. 'Jeems thinks Jericho's great. He's all like *'that Jericho is grand, he is,* and *I'd love ter have Jericho come along, but he'd slow us up so he would,'* Benjamin stopped.

Will laughed. 'Nice accent.' His voice took on a more serious tone. 'What do you think about Jericho?'

'Well,' Benjamin screwed up his nose. 'I'm not really sure. Don't get me wrong, he's been really nice to me. Like super nice. But, I don't know, there's just something about his that makes me feel a bit uneasy. Maybe it's just the way he looks.'

'Could be,' Will countered. 'Everyone around here seems to think he's alright.'

'Must just be me,' Benjamin shrugged. 'I've never been much good at judging people.'

'I don't know. My grandmother's never said too much about him. And normally if she has real strong feelings about someone, good or bad, she'd let me know.'

Benjamin yawned. 'Well, whatever. It doesn't matter anyways. He's been nice enough to me - given me some stuff.'

'Really?'

'Nothing big. Just like little trinkets and stuff. He gave me a piece of glass he said was like really special.'

'That sounds strange. I'm gonna ask my grandmother if she knows about any special glass.'

'Well, like I said we'll be leaving soon. Maybe even tomorrow so I better get to bed.'

Will got up to walk Benjamin back. 'Don't worry, I know the way.'

'It's about time,' Will joked.

'Ha. You're funny. See ya later.'

'See ya.'

Benjamin walked down the corridor, his feet padding softly against the ground. He didn't really know why he told Will about the green piece of glass Jericho had given him. He said it would bring luck, like a four leaf clover. Benjamin had smiled politely and took it, not really thinking of it again until a few minutes ago.

He turned the corner but pulled back quickly when a figure came out from a small opening in the wall just ahead of him. Peering around the corner he saw Hubrice in the torchlight, checking both ways before he strode off in the opposite direction.

With Hubrice out of sight, his heart sped up as he approached the crack that the big man had just squeezed out of. What was he doing in there? And how did he manage to get through such a small crack? Excitement flowed through him as he pushed through the small gap. He stopped a few times, convinced he heard movement in the corridor. He pushed through until he came to an open space. Then his blood went cold as a hand gripped his right shoulder.

Another hand over his mouth. 'It's just me,' Will whispered.

'What are you doing here?' Benjamin took Will's hand away from his mouth and turned to face him.

'I came after you to say you can come and have breakfast with me and my grandmother tomorrow if you wanted.' Will dropped his hand from Benjamin's shoulder. 'What are *you* doing here?'

'I was just heading back to my hovel when I saw Hubrice come out of here.'

'Really?' Will answered. 'I never knew about this place. What is it?'

'I don't know, but I'm going to find out.' He groped around for a torch and, lighting it with the flint Will had given him, looked around.

The strong smell of sulphur hung in the air. Smoke rose from the candles that dotted the room.

'Should we light some?' Benjamin asked feebly, his knees weak.

'Better not risk it,' Will whispered. 'This way, if we hear someone coming we can just blow out the torch.'

Benjamin nodded. 'Look at all this stuff.'

Both boys slowly went around the walls of the small chamber, covered with pictures and newspapers clippings. Benjamin's eyes floated over a sea of faces before resting on a newspaper clipping of a group of young men and women standing in front of some kind of shop.

'Look here, Will,' he read the names out underneath the photo. '*Amethy, Diamia, Iustitia,* who are these people?'

Will came up behind Benjamin and scanned the yellowed clipping. 'Iustitia was Hubrice's father. He looks young there. I suppose the rest of them are his sisters.'

'How do you know so much about Hubrice's family?' Benjamin asked, slightly suspicious.

'I told you, my grandmother tells me everything. She knew Hubrice's father *and* grandfather.' Will noticed Benjamin's impressed look. 'She's 115 years old, ya know.'

Benjamin let out a low whistle. 'I never thought anybody could live that long.'

'Meridia used to be such a great place to live that everyone lived for a really long time.' Will turned and moved to the back wall.

'I am definitely going to be talking to your grandmother,' Benjamin stated.

Will didn't respond right away. 'I suppose it'll be okay. She's been asking me when I'm going to bring you around anyways. I think she knows that we've been hanging out after hours.' Something caught his eye. 'No way! Look at this.'

Following Will to the back of the small chamber, a tall, thick piece of stone stood on a thick oak desk. The only piece of furniture in the room, the desk was pushed up against the back wall so the large tablet could lean against it. Benjamin brought the torch closer, where four candles stood in a row directly below the stone tablet.

'There's something on it, but I can't see it very well.' Will took the torch and lit the four candles on the desk. The chamber lit up.

Broken at the top and bottom, the stone tablet was full of intricate carvings. A thin tree trunk ran all the way up the middle, with four heads spaced evenly along it, their facial features as clear as if they were photos. Names were etched under each face. Smaller branches ran off to the side of each head, with smaller ones running out of them. Along the smallest branches were small banners with names of various people.

'What is it?' Benjamin asked Will as they studied the carvings.

'It's Hubrice's family tree.'

Benjamin looked at it a bit more. 'Kind of weird, don't you think. Those heads look like they're on a wooden pole.'

'They're not,' snapped Will. 'That's a tree trunk.' He ran his finger up the centre towards the top of the tablet. 'Those are branches are off to the side.'

'Oh, yeah. I get it now.' Benjamin looked closer.

'I've heard of these before,' Will said, mainly to himself.

'Let me guess, your grandmother?'

'No. Jericho, actually.' Will shook his head, not taking his eyes of the tablet. 'He said they're really rare. You see where it's broken off,' he pointed to the bottom. 'Well, from here down was probably loads more, and the trunk would have been thicker the further down it got. Jericho said the tablets were all made from the same stone, but in four generation chunks.'

'These big heads creep me out,' Benjamin read the names aloud. 'It starts with Veratio, then Probitus, Iustitia, Hubrice. What about Hubrice's kids? Where's the top?'

'Well, I guess Hubrice is the top. Only the oldest gets to be in the middle, so maybe he broke it off when Jasper died. Who knows?' Will shrugged. 'Anyways, Jericho told me that he always suspected Hubrice would have one. It's called Horatio's Ledger. He said there has only ever been one real set, and that the base of it, the first one, started with a guy named Horatio. Apparently his family is the only one that has the real ledgers. As more children are born, then more tablets are made. This Horatio guy is on the first one. Jericho reckons that on the first tablet Horatio is carved

189

lying down with the tree coming right out of his stomach.'

'Ugh,' Benjamin said in disgust. He turned his attention back to the tablet. 'Man these names are weird. *Veratio, Tegrit, Probitus*. You couldn't make these up.'

Benjamin leaned on the desk, his right hand on a pile of dusty papers. As they toppled over, he lurched forward to catch them, causing the candles to rock uneasily in their holders.

Will caught his arm. 'Watch it! You're gonna burn the place down.' Benjamin used the shadows to hide a scowl. Rearranging the pile, something caught his eye.

Tucked underneath the stack of papers was a green leather bound book with ornate gold drawing along the border. He fished it out and started flicking through the pages.

'Will, look. It's like some sort of scrapbook,'

Will peered over his shoulder. 'This should be good. Hubrice's father used to be the mayor of the village they were from, so they were always in the papers.' Benjamin tenderly turned the pages, exposing various letters from Hubrice's wife, newspaper clippings of his family, and old speeches from when his father was mayor. The middle of the book held a small bundle of old papers folded in to each other.

'These are all loose in here.' He gingerly fingered through them. 'I think they're about when Jasper died.'

'No, look, there's a letter on top,' Will unfolded the piece of paper and read it outloud.

My dearest Probitus,

As you read this, I could very well be taking my last breath. I don't write this to haunt you, but to let you know I am truly at the end of my time. It is my dying hope that we can once and for all put our differences aside for the sake of your mother, who misses you terribly. I hear your lovely wife, Ruby is with child once again, and I will make it my last prayer for you to have the son you always wanted and whom is so desperately needed to continue our rich line of anointed leaders. I beg you remember the oracle that was spoken of the one who will finally send Howl to his grave. You know that we believe this person can only come from our blood line. Although I dare not ask Gideon, it is sure, as it would follow a long line of rulers and anointed dignitaries. Our parting was bitter after the birth of your third daughter, and for my actions I can only apologise and beg your forgiveness. Only time will make you realise how desperate Meridia is, and I fear we are to see further destruction of our beautiful land. The oracle, I am told, speaks of a boy although my source may not be reliable and further attempts have not been successful (as you know).

Be strong, my son. Do your best to resist whatever Howl may throw at you, for he is cunning and as of now is using his servant Magh more and more. There are many who would not believe she is from him but Gideon is certain and from his lips comes truth. Try your utmost to listen to the part of your heart that is strong and honourable, and do not make the mistakes of your father, who became weak, with dire consequences. Listen to Gideon, no matter how difficult things may become, and may I see you again in spirit.

Yours in parting,

Father.

They both turned back to the stone tablet. 'If this letter was to Probitus,' Benjamin's voice trailed off.

'Then that means that this was from his father Veratio,' Will finished. 'Wow, this is really old. Probitus was Hubrice's grandfather so Vertio would have been his great grandfather.'

'Cool.' Benjamin said. He put the letter aside. 'Look, there's an article about what happened to Jasper.' Straining his eyes, he read it aloud:

Akin Durst, leader of the Potens party has made a general call to find their next leader. 'We've been drifting for too long,' Durst said today in an early morning, hastily called press conference. 'We feel it's time to let fate decide our next leader. Apparently an oracle exists, but no one has ever been able to raise it, and time is being wasted.' Durst explained with a smile. 'If I'm honest, I'm not sure there even is one. But, the Potens party will need a leader and we need to take action.'

As most Meridians will know, the last line of Horatio died out, and although there have been claims to his line in the past, it's never been proven.

'That line has been lost, and it's time to reclaim it. We're sure that the real line of Horatio is out there somewhere. Meridia is depending on us to find him,' commented Durst this morning.

'So we've issued an open invitation to all those who have a son born this year to contact us. Our advisors are currently working on a special oil that will tell us once and for all who the rightful leader is. The oil will have to be rubbed in to the child's head at night. The child who truly is from the lost line of Horatio will have gold dust where the oil was the night previous.'

This announcement comes with hot debate, even within the ranks of the opposition. Shortly after the announcement, senior opposition leaders met in a secret location to discuss the impact of such a bold move by the Potens. The discussions broke down and party loyalty became split, with leader Hubrice Lack walking out, declaring his intention to seek the oil for his newly born son, Jasper. 'This is what we've all been waiting for,' Lack commented in front of his home earlier this afternoon. 'Meridia has been without a rightful line of rulers for far too long. The Lack family has always claimed to be the last remaining line of Horatio, and now is our chance to prove it.'

Deputy opposition leader Samson Pringle warns against the tactics. 'This is nothing more than a man hunt. It is not up to Durst or his ill-advised party to choose Meridia's rightful leader. Nothing good will come of this. My most trusted advisor assured me that the leader will be made known when the time is right. I urge everyone to resist this gloryfest. The choice has already been made by forces beyond our control.'

This comes while hundreds prepare to queue to collect the oil, said to be worth its weight in gold. Claims the opposition make are dismissed by Durst. 'It's all fear-mongering,' he replies hotly. 'Your son

194

will either wake up covered in gold dust or not, it's that simple.'

'What a bafoon,' Will said quickly.

Benjamin re-read the article. 'So the Potens party-'

'They're the ones who ended up being associated with Magh. After this all kicked off, it was clear that most of the party were Raptors or Tatty's.'

'And they were leading Meridia?'

'I know, crazy, eh?'

Benjamin read on. 'I wonder who Samson Pringle is.'

'Your uncle, I think,' Will responded. 'I'm sure my grandmother said that Samson Pringle and everyone opposed tried to block roads and everything to stop the oil from being handed out. But it didn't work.'

'But when you look at the letter from Hubrice's great grandfather,' Benjamin commented and picked up the old piece of parchment. 'This family was under a lot of pressure.'

'I bet Hubrice was first in line to get that oil,' Will scoffed and looked around some more. Benjamin kept looking at the book.

'Just a minute though,' Benjamin said and swung his hand around to pick up another piece of paper. His hand hit one of the candle holders and the candle came down quickly, catching on the dry, dusty papers. The other candles followed and in seconds the desk was engulfed in flames. Benjamin jumped back, bumping in to Will who hit the wall with the torch in his hand, setting the wall hangings on fire.

'We got to get out of here! Benjamin, come on!'

Benjamin's feet seemed rooted to the spot. He looked around in disbelief. Without thinking, he plunged his hands in to the flames on the desk to retrieve the scrapbook before Will grabbed him by the collar.

'C'mon, we got to get back before someone comes,' Will gasped, choking on the thick smoke.

Squeezing through, the two boys tumbled out in to the corridor, flames licking their heels. 'Let's go,' Will said, but it was too late. Benjamin looked up to see Jeems running towards him. He turned his head the opposite direction to see Hubrice, a crazed look on his face, making ground quickly, shouting and ranting. Behind Hubrice were a few men with buckets of water.

Will managed to scramble to his feet before Benjamin, who was struggling to stand on his weakened legs, the book held tightly in his arms. Suddenly Benjamin felt two huge hands grab him and his feet left the floor. He was whipped around, coming nose to nose with an enraged Hubrice Lack.

'You filthy little low-life!' Hubrice roared, showering Benjamin with his spit. 'How dare you. After everything,' Hubrice stopped talking and began to shake Benjamin violently, his head whipping back and forth. The book left his hands and dropped to the ground. Then he jerked forwards as Hubrice tumbled to the ground.

'That's enough, Hubrice. Let 'im go!' Jeems, much shorter than Hubrice, had rushed him at the knees. Jeems recovered quickly and pulled Benjamin up by the shoulders, narrowly missing a swipe from Hubrice.

'He's a filthy troublemaker!' Hubrice roared from the ground. 'He's going to pay!'

'He's just bein' a kid!' Jeems retorted. 'And if ya think he hasn't paid enough fer his life, then walk a mile in his shoes.'

'Get him out of here! Get him out of my sight!' Hubrice had a look in his eye that Benjamin did not trust, and he knew by the expression on Jeems' face that he didn't trust it either.

'C'mon, let's get ya outta here,' Jeems held Benjamin up as he pushed through the crowd that had gathered.

Benjamin stumbled along. 'The bo- the,'

'Don't worry 'bout anything right now, let's get ya outta here,' Jeems said gruffly. With tremendous strength Jeems ushered Benjamin along, coughing and spitting.

He tried his best, but his feet just wouldn't catch up to him. 'I didn't – I sorry – I –' Benjamin was caught in another coughing fit, his chest tight and heavy.

'Stop tryin' ter talk, ya've got too much smoke inside ya, so ya do,' Jeems spoke sternly but softly to Benjamin as he carried him over his shoulder through the main room and up the tunnel towards Mrs Peabody's house.

14

The Powers of Mrs Peabody

The acrid smell of burning dust and paper behind them, Benjamin found his feet as they walked through the gate in to Mrs Peabody's back garden. Primrose greeted them, her wet tongue sliding across their faces.

'Down, girl,' Jeems ordered, sending Primrose in a sulk. 'She must've heard the noise, I s'pose,' he reasoned. Then he chuckled and stopped. 'She's missed ya, so she has.'

Unable to hold back, she nudged Benjamin with her snout. 'That and she loves fire,' he said, watching her lick the thick black marks off Benjamin's face.

The quip tree, insulated by a layer of ice; the acrid smell of smoke; the blue-black sky; they all swirled around Benjamin's head as he stood there, his teeth chattering, leaning on Primrose for support. The cold made his nostrils stick together and through his blurred vision could see steam rising from his mouth.

Giving in, he fell to his knees, sinking down in to the thick layer of snow that lay all around. He recognised the outline of Mrs Peabody coming across the garden, a concerned look on her face and a blanket in her arms. As she approached Primrose backed off. She knelt in front of him, looking directly in to his eyes. He got lost in them; eyes that said *I know you didn't mean it,* eyes that comforted and consoled. She threw the blanket over and embraced him. Warmth returned to his body and he stayed there, not holding back the tears that came.

It was the rustle of the trees that broke the silence.

'We should get him inside,' Mrs Peabody said to Jeems. Jeems studied the overhanging treetops for a moment before nodding. Benjamin felt Mrs Peabody pick him up, her arms wrapped snugly around him. He felt as if he were floating. He didn't understand the feeling that had come over him. It was as if he was asleep but awake at the same time. Although he could hear the conversations around him, it was as if they were happening far away. He had given up trying to look around, and let his body relax in her arms.

They were inside now, the door creaking open. Footsteps, then chairs scraping along the floor. He lay in her lap, another force taking control of his body as images of what happened churned around in his head. Then gradually, his thoughts evaporated in to puffs of white smoke, until nothing was left but a light; the softest of glows that grew until it filled his entire mind. It was like he was under the power of something that he could not resist; something he did not want to resist.

Like a whirlwind, silvery strands twisted and blew until they formed a lions' face. It came close in front of him, the animal's warm breath against his lips. His eyes, so close, showed endless kindness, not what Benjamin expected from such a ferocious beast. The lion's mane extended beyond vision, his tawny hair looked both soft and coarse.

It stayed there, in Benjamin's mind until, without warning, it gently bit the collar of his shirt and carried him off. He climbed on its massive back, its height frightening but safe. At first the lion walked, then ran effortlessly. It gained speed, almost as if they were flying. And then they were flying; running in the air by sheer power. They climbed high above Meridia, and it was all passing by him – fields and forests, rivers and mountains. They came to rest on the peak of the tallest mountain. Marcus and Riley were there waiting.

'We've been waiting for you, mate.' Marcus said with a smile.

'This is so cool,' Riley added. 'But we miss you.'

Benjamin's eyes filled with tears. Marcus spoke up. 'Do what you've got to do, mate. Only you can do this. You've got lots of backup, but that doesn't mean you won't have to fight. Sometimes our biggest enemies are ourselves.'

Before Benjamin could speak, Marcus and Riley gave Benjamin a hug before walking down the mountainside, disappearing in to mist.

The lion sat next to Benjamin, inviting him to look around. He could see Water's Hyde in the distance, along with the forest and the clearing with the stone markers. Everything was covered with light, except for a patch off to the right that was covered in darkness. He studied the dark area, a tiny speck on the landscape. As he looked at it, it got closer, the speck growing larger, like it was coming towards him, or he was going towards it. Eventually it was right in front of him until he could see through the darkness. Smoke rose from a small mountain covered in the darkness; there was a deep chill in the air. It came so he could see inside the mountain where beasts crawled in and out of caves, scaling the walls.

Outside the caves were high thorned bushes with more beasts climbing through them. He heard Magh laughing; it made him tense up. As fast as it came, the darkness zoomed away, disappearing back to a speck over to the far right. The lion nuzzled in to Benjamin's neck. It was time to go. The lion ran down the mountain, surefooted and quick. On through fields and forest until they came upon a desert. On they went, the sun scorching Benjamin, making him tired and dry.

'Stop,' he gasped, but the lion continued. The sand burned his eyes and was gritty in his mouth. Suddenly they plunged in to water. It was refreshing and clear as they went deeper. Benjamin kept drinking the water, feeling refreshed. Strangely, he didn't feel breathless and his lungs were not wanting air. Fish with scales like rainbows swam around and over them, using the waves to propel them further. The lion swam to the surface, to where ice was floating on the water. They continued to swim through the ice floes. Benjamin could see his breath in the cold air as they manoeuvred masterfully through the chunks of fast flowing ice. To their right a strong undercurrent threatened to pull them in. To the left, an enormous crocodile was swimming towards them. Fear rose up in him. The lion was aware of the monster but did not pay attention to it. He kept swimming as the beast snapped and swished around them, never coming close enough to harm them. They crawled up the icy bank and onto the snow. The lion dried Benjamin off with his giant mane and laid him to rest under the stars that were dancing in the sky.

'Dog's need a break!' Jeems called out. Benjamin's eyes fluttered open. Lying on his back looking up at the midnight sky, thick ribbons of light danced between the stars that dotted it. White, blue and pink hues dove and leapt effortlessly through the darkness. Looking on either side, he realised he was fixed to a sled that was being dragged through the snow. Taymar was beside him on snowshoes, the powdery snow flying up and falling gracefully to the sides. A team of dogs hitched like reindeer were pulling the sled he was on. To his left Jeems was on another sled, standing at the back expertly guiding his dog team around the snow drifts. The dogs slowed down. His brain ticking he managed to piece together bits of what happened after he left the Exiles. He recalled his encounter with the lion, then the other memories came back – the fire, Hubrice's hands around his throat. He shuddered and drove them out of his mind. The sled came to a stop.

'Jeems?' Benjamin struggled to get up from under his heavy blankets.

'Oh, ya've decided ter join us, have ya?' Jeems said playfully. 'Good ter 'ave ya back, anyways. Y'awright?'

'I think so.' He put his hand to his throat and winced. 'If I could – just – get out.' Taymar stood over Benjamin and hoisted him up with both hands.

'There you are, little warrior,' she replied, half laughing. She threw him a pair of snowshoes. 'You'll need these if you don't want to sink all the way up to your neck.'

'They're snowshoes,' Jeems noticed the confused look on Benjamin's face. 'Just put yer foot in like so.' Benjamin copied and eventually managed to strap the snowshoes onto his boots.

He soon realised that walking in snowshoes was not easy, and he fell three times before taking more than two steps.

'Where are we?' He asked, noticing a small building up ahead. It had a huge satellite dish perched off to the side, with a small house attached to the back of the building.

'Well, we're North, as ya can see,' replied Jeems. He untied each dog from its harness and unpacked the sled. The dogs, not bothered by the cold, gathered around bowls of food Taymar had put out for them.

'Get off the sled, Primrose!' Jeems tried to push the little dragon off. 'I told ya, Batar has a special spot for ya in his garage, so he does. It'll be nice an' warm in there, so it will.' Unlike the dogs, Primrose didn't like the cold. She sat on the sled, shivering, icicles hanging from both her nostrils. 'Yer such a baby,' Jeems chortled, shaking his head. 'Go on up ter Batar's. Let 'im know we're here an' ya can go find somewheres warm.'

Reluctantly, Primrose got off the sled and made motion to fly. Her frozen wings crinkled open, and she flew low to the ground, hugging herself.

'This 'ere's Batar's house,' Jeems turned back to Benjamin. 'He lives 'ere with his wife, Sasha. They're both researchers. There ain't nothing they don't know about what goes on up 'ere I tell ya.'

Benjamin watched Primrose knocking on a window of the house and waving. 'So they're like scientists?'

Jeems nodded. 'They'll be able ter help us track the next league. Or at least they'll be able to help us steer clear of Sqwal.'

'Is Sqwal some kind of mutated crocodile?' Benjamin asked, thinking back to his strange dream with the lion.

Jeems looked impressed and nodded. 'That's wot I've heard, anyways. How did ya figure that one out so quickly?'

'Lucky guess, I suppose.'

'Is it?' Taymar came up to them. 'Or has your time under the power been helpful? There is more to Mrs Peabody then red lipstick.'

Benjamin opened his mouth to reply but never got the chance. Just then they heard a loud whoop from the house and saw a slender man waving to them. They picked up their bags and started towards the open door.

Stumbling across the snow, Benjamin thought about what Taymar had said. *Under the power.* What did she mean? He couldn't deny that his latest dream was unlike any he had ever had. It was so vivid and real, and it wasn't like he was asleep, really. Come to think of it, it did feel like he was under some sort of power. All he knew was that, given the chance, he would do it again.

Caught in his thoughts, Benjamin tread on the back of Jeems' snowshoe as he stopped short before the house.

'Sorry,' Benjamin mumbled, avoiding Jeems' frown.

'Finally you come!' The tall, slender man stood in the doorway of the house, pulling on his winter coat and boots. 'Sasha!' The man called in to an intercom system that was on the wall. He started jabbering away in a different language, his beard grazing the speaker. He shot a smile at the three as he bounced out to greet them. The bitter cold met with the warmth of the house and caused steam to rise from the door.

'You get lost?' Batar asked Jeems.

'Nah, just had a bit of a run-in is all. Sorry ter worry ya.'

'Is okay. You here now.' He turned to Benjamin and pointed to himself. 'Batar,' he said. His ginger beard and moustache carried a hint of icicles around his mouth. 'You are Benjamin?'

Benjamin nodded. Batar took his bags and carried them in to the house. 'Come and get warm. I put dogs away.' Just then a tall slender woman with very short blonde hair came through the door.

'Sasha,' Batar held out his hand and introduced the woman. He spoke to her in the same foreign language he used before. Sasha put her thick parka and boots on and nodded. Batar put his arm around her. 'My wife Sasha,' he announced. But it seemed as though the only stranger was Benjamin, because she immediately hugged Jeems and kissed Taymar hello.

Once inside, Jeems, Taymar and Sasha chatted in the same language Batar had spoke earlier while Benjamin found a seat by the fire. A large polar bear skin lay on the floor, its head almost as big as Primroses', its eyes beady and threatening. Benjamin studied if for a few moments, unable to resist the urge to stroke it. The thick fur was coarse and strong, much different then it looked.

'It dead,' Sasha came over to Benjamin, who jumped back quickly. Sasha giggled and knelt down over the creature. 'We – found – it-' her eyes went from side to side and she waved her hand in front of her. Benjamin looked at her strangely.

'Was it dead when you found it?' Benjamin finally asked.

'Yah.' Sasha nodded her head enthusiastically. 'My English not – good,' she stumbled.

'Oh, that's okay, I hardly understand what anybody's talking about around here anyways.' He looked at Sasha's totally lost expressed. 'I suppose you didn't understand that. It's okay,' Benjamin called out.

'She's Russian, not deaf,' Jeems chipped in as he and Taymar walked in to the room with steaming mugs. 'Ya don' have ter shout.'

'Well, I didn't know,' Benjamin shot back. 'It's not like anyone told me I was going to have to speak Russian.'

'Suppose not,' Jeems sat down beside Benjamin and tussled his hair.

'How come Batar can speak English so well?'

Jeems shrugged. 'Just caught on, I s'pose. People up 'round 'ere didn't really think they needed ter speak another language, I s'pose. But now with not many left, it's harder to find any'un who doesn't speak English, so it is.'

Just then Batar came back in the house. 'Dogs good,' he called out. 'Them and Primrose eating some whale meat.' He looked at Benjamin. 'What?'

'You caught a whale?' Benjamin choked.

'We don't hunt, we try and save animals,' Batar picked up a mug and sat down on the polar bear rug with Sasha. 'That whale, and this bear, both died of hunger. There's nothing left for them to eat,' Batar looked at Jeems and Taymar as he said this, like he was pleading a case.

'There's no doubt of it, Batar. Meridia's in a bad way,' Jeems responded. 'It's everywhere, but it's gonna get better, so it will.'

'We hope.' Batar huffed.

'So what do you do up here?' Benjamin asked.

'Research,' Sasha answered, smiling broadly.

Batar nodded. 'We track animals. Where they go, what they eat. If Magh tries to get them, we will know.'

'So are you safe up here?' Benjamin asked. 'What if the bedruggers come to the house?'

Batar laughed out loud and said something in Russian. 'Those cowards! They have thin skin.' He mocked them shivering. 'Too cold, too cold,' he laughed again and tapped Sasha on the back before translating what he had said. After he was finished, Sasha giggled.

'Well, it is pretty cold up here,' Benjamin reasoned.

'That good,' Batar answered. He stoked the fire and added another log. 'Keeps them away.' He played with the fire for a while before Sasha said something to him. 'Sasha asks, what you are doing here? Gideon tells us you come, but he didn't say why.'

The three friends looked at each other. Batar continued. 'We are happy you here. But why?'

Jeems spoke up first. 'We gotta get ter Sqwal.'

Even Sasha understood Jeems. She drew in breath as Batar dropped the fire poker.

'What you mean, you get to Sqwal?' Batar looked from Jeems to Taymar. 'What do you think it is? A puppy!? Why you talking such- how you say – rubbish?'

'There is no mistake,' Taymar explained. Sqwal is guarding one of the leagues that Benjamin needs to help him complete his task.'

Batar shook his head. 'Sqwal guards nothing! It eats everything. No, you make mistake. What is this, this league?'

The response was left until Batar could translate the conversation to Sasha, who had become quite anxious at the mention of Sqwal.

'It's the next thing I have to find,' Benjamin piped up. He noticed the sideways looks exchanged by Jeems and Taymar. 'You know, to try and save Meridia from Magh, or Howl, or – whoever.' His cheeks grew hot. Jeems always made it sound so much better.

'Ah! I know what you talk about now,' Batar jumped up. 'Wait a minute.' He ran out of the room and was heard rummaging around in another part of the house before returning with a large rolled up piece of paper.

'This is what you talk about,' he said enthusiastically and spread the page out on the floor. The rest of the group crowded around him, the light from the fire and oil lamps creating shadows off the walls.

Various sketches and writings covered the scroll. All of the sketches had scientific measurements around it, with some complicated formulas that Benjamin decided he was never going to understand. The one sketch showed a huge iceberg off the coast jammed against a cliff that jutted out from the shore. Next to it was the same iceberg but titled 'BACK VIEW'. It looked the same but at the bottom was an underground cave in the iceberg. Near the cave was an arrow pointing towards it, with words next to it that read: *entrance*.

'You don't want Sqwal, you want this,' Batar explained. 'This is where you go for next league, no?' He looked up. Jeems and Taymar nodded.

'But ol' Sqwal'll be 'round somewheres, won't he?' Jeems asked.

213

Batar leaned his head to one side and shrugged. 'Hard to say. It lives very deep in ocean. Deeper than any machine can go.'

'But it will know to expect us, surely,' Taymar added.

Batar puffed his chest out. 'How? Noone comes up here. There has been no tracks, maybe a few wolves.'

'All the same, I wouldn't put my harpoon away, so I wouldn't,' Jeems replied.

Batar laughed. 'Harpoon won't help you fight Sqwal,' he rocked on his knees, translating to Sasha who nodded somberly.

'Why?' Benjamin asked.

'Why what?' Batar stopped laughing.

'Why wouldn't a harpoon work?'

Batar fixed Benjamin with a steely look. 'Because whale has soft skin, Sqwal has thick scales. Like little dragon, but twice – three times as thick. And it is huge, bigger than largest whale in ocean. It has head almost as big as house, and most of that is mouth with sharp teeth – four rows.'

Sasha turned the paper over to show Benjamin a sketch of some deep sea monster. The three drew closer to the sketch while Batar continued.

'This just rough drawing. No one knows what Sqwal looks like. No one has got close enough to get good look. Well, if they have got close they don't make it back.'

The air got chilly, despite the fire that burned so close to him. His eyes followed the drawing – the V-shaped mouth with four rows of teeth, four front fangs that protruded at the front. Three sets of six eyes were positioned on top and either side of its huge head. It had a short, thick neck that led to a broad back covered with spiky scales, both longer and sharper than Primrose's. It had two huge front flippers with three claws at the joint in the middle of them. Its short legs folded neatly against its body for swimming, but the claws on it were not small. The rest of its body looked like sheer muscle, with a tail that resembled one of a whale but with a deadly stinger at the end.

'That's Sqwal?' Benjamin asked weakly.

Batar nodded. 'This just rough. Like I said, nobody ever seen Sqwal close up to know for sure. I drew this from old writings of creature.' Batar turned the page over again to reveal the scribbling in the bottom corner. Benjamin strained to read it.

Sasha giggled. 'Not e-englesh,' she shook her head and patted his hand. Benjamin looked in to her blue eyes. He smiled back.

'So ya reckon we may be able ter do this without runnin' inter Sqwal, do ya Batar?' Jeems asked.

'Possible, but not 100%. We track lots of marine life around there. Most things we lose track of are narwhals. Sqwal gets them. It breathes underwater, so no need to come to surface.' Batar got quiet. 'I saw it only once.'

Everyone reacted at the same time. Taymar and Jeems' raised their eyebrows curiously, Benjamin drew breath sharply, and Sasha sat silently, tears falling from her cheeks.

'Three years back, I go across to check on baby seals that lost mother. Then ice rumbled under my feet. I was shocked – I think – what's going on? Ice should be still thick. But ice keep rumbling so I got back on sled and get dogs to hurry back across ice. When I a mile or so away, I heard huge crash. I turned and Sqwal had broke through three, four feet ice. It crashed about, a blue whale in mouth.

'Did it see you?' Benjamin gasped.

Batar shook his head. 'It smelled dogs first. When it ate whale, I thought, good, it will go. But it stayed, sniffing towards us, smelling dogs. Then it screeched so loud I had to cover my ears.' Batar put his hands to his ears. 'Dogs went mad. They took off and I had just time to grab hold of sled but was knocked off. Then Sqwal went underwater and I thought she would come for us. I was dragging behind sled, hitting chunks of hard snow.' Batar lifted up his shirt to show a huge gash that ran down the length of his torso. 'This is where I hit a chunk of ice. It tore right through my coat.' He hugged Sasha before continuing. 'I heard banging underneath me, far down and I knew that I had come to place where ice too thick even for Sqwal, but still went on until I knew we were on land.'

'Ya ne'er told me that before, Batar,' Jeems said softly.

Batar shrugged. 'We don't see each other much. When we do I want it to be happy times.'

Jeems nodded slowly and sat down next to Benjamin who was eyeing the sketch. 'We got ya past Er, didn't we?' He spoke softly. 'We'll get past Sqwal, so we will. Ya just need ter set yer mind ter wot ya gotta do, an' that's gettin' the league in the Arcrux. Nuthin' else. Ya hear?'

Benjamin nodded numbly, knowing he would have to fight for his life before he reached the league.

Taymar took over translating for Sasha, which sped things up a bit. They talked about their next steps, Taymar translating quietly, stopping only to add her own thoughts or relay Sasha's. It turned out that Sasha was extremely clever and knowledgeable about the area. She had also devised a breathing technique that allowed her to stay underwater for longer than most people.

'It would be good for you to learn this from Sasha, little warrior,' Taymar commented. 'Once you get in to the iceberg you may find air, but you will have to swim around to the opening, and it is difficult to tell how deep down it actually is.'

Batar nodded. 'A huge rocky cliff sits against the iceberg, right where the opening is. Maybe Gideon's idea of a joke,' they all chuckled.

'Or summat else ter deter others from gettin' at it,' Jeems responded.

'That reminds me,' Batar lit up. He went from the room again and came back with an old, dusty book, its thick yellowed pages covered with faded handwriting. 'This is journal of great explorer that lived long ago. I remember reading part where he got to opening for iceberg.' Batar flipped through the pages gingerly. 'Okay, here it is. Wait, I need to read and then translate to English.'

After a few moments Batar continued. 'Okay, he says, *At long last, after many hours of planning, I finally managed to get to the entrance of the one iceberg that is said to hold the ice fountain. The water under the iceberg is the coldest I have ever felt, and I found myself coming up for warmth a few times, even with my diving gear on. The entrance is wedged between the rocks, with the opening too small to go through with air tanks, so they had to be taken off and brought back to the boat. This made it all the more difficult, and I was getting anxious at how long I was in the water, not only because of Sqwal but of all the other creatures that would like to have me for their dinner. Had I not been sure that Sqwal had just had three orcas and a beluga whale I would not have risked it, but I have waited so long to finally put together the riddles the desperation would have killed me if not the creature. Going back to the opening was harder every time, with the current increasing around it, almost trying to keep me out. In the end I had to grab hold of the rocks as best I could to keep from being taken in by the current and spat out to sea. After struggling down to the entrance it was to my utter disappointment to find that it was blocked by a thick sheet of ice. Ice so clear I*

219

didn't know it was there, and in my excitement swam directly in to it. There is definitely a chamber inside the iceberg, but what is in there or how one gets in I did not find out on this expedition. I only had a few minutes to try and break through the ice with anything I could find on the boat – I tried an axe and shovel but they didn't even make a mark on the thick frozen door. I will have to go back when I invent something that will cut through the door, or respect the very meaning of it that intruders are not welcome. It seems that the oracle is true, there is only one that is intended to enter and I am not it.'

'So did he try again?' Benjamin asked.

Batar passed the journal to Sasha so she could read it herself. 'He doesn't write about trying it again. That was near the end of journal. His son writes on next few pages that his father went out in blizzard one day and never returned.'

'Lost in a storm? No?' Jeems said in disbelief.

Batar shrugged. 'I imagine so. It is not hard. You must be always ready for storms here. If not, you will freeze to death out there.'

'It sounds like loads of people knew about the oracle,' Benjamin said out loud.

'Many knew about the oracle,' Taymar replied, 'but none of them knew what was in the oracle. As you know, that was protected.'

'So how did so many people know it even existed?' Benjamin asked.

'The Bogwumps were not always protected by the mist that covers their bog,' Taymar answered, dodging a glare from Jeems. 'There was a time when they roamed freely around Meridia, travelling to the far reaches of Meridia. Many times Gideon would send them out to give people messages from him. Some were good messages, some were warnings. Most of them told people what their future would be like if they continued to follow Howl. Some messages were about giving people hope. One of the messages that gave people hope, little warrior, is the promise that one day one of their own will come to save them.'

'So why do they live in the mist now?'

'Because, some of the people in Meridia took to evil ways,' Taymar answered. Jeems shifted uncomfortably in his seat. Batar and Sasha left the room, mumbling something about having to cook dinner. 'They did not focus on the message the Bogwumps brought, but were jealous that Gideon used the Bogwumps and not them. What they didn't understand is that Gideon gives different people

221

different abilities. But many didn't see it that way. They thought it was a power that could be transferred to them. Some plotted to capture the Bogwumps and steal their power to see into the future. They did not understand that it was not power, but a gift given to them. Bogwumps could only see what Gideon wanted them to see.'

'Gideon told me that they needed to be protected,' Benjamin remarked.

'Come. Eat,' Sasha called out from the other room. They perched themselves on stools and picked away at the variety of foods that Batar and Sasha cooked for them.

'Eat. Is good,' Batar pushed a plate of food towards Benjamin. Nothing on it looked familiar.

'Eat. Is good for you,' Batar encouraged Benjmain. 'Puts hair on your chest,' he looked at Jeems who laughed and shook his head.

'What is this?' Benjamin picked up what looked like a small octopus with his forefinger and thumb. It dangled tenderly, suspended a few inches above his plate.

'Squid,' Sasha replied with a smile. She put something else on Benjamin's plate that looked equally unfamiliar.

'What's that?' Benjamin's question took on a horrified tone.

Jeems leaned over. 'Ketchup. Just try it, ya never know wot yer gonna think o' it until ya do.'

Benjamin closed his eyes and took a mouthful. Amazed that he didn't feel sick, he kept picking at his food, joining in to the laughter, eating more bread than anything else.

15

Spies

Benjamin rested his wind chaffed face against the pillow. Sasha and Batar had many spare bedrooms in their house. 'There is a lot of room to build big house,' Batar joked earlier.

Riley and Marcus popped in to his head. If Marcus knew about Meridia all along, did that mean Riley knew too? No, he couldn't. Riley came to Hadley Priest after he did, even if he did just turn up one day without any notice. Not even Hester seemed to know anything about Riley coming. But that's not saying much; Hester never knows what's going on around the house. Benjamin chuckled and snuggled in to the furry blanket, thinking about the iceberg he needed to get in to. If a grown man with experience at diving couldn't get through the thick sheet of ice, he didn't stand a chance.

Slipping in to sleep, he had a dream. He dreamed he was under water, swimming downwards alongside a huge chunk of ice. The water was getting colder as he went deeper. Eventually he found the door and could see a chamber beyond it. He started to bang on the door but he couldn't break through. His lungs ached for breath. He kept banging, not wanting to go up for air, afraid he would fail. Too weak to continue, his hand dropped to his side, and as he was slipping down to the depths, he saw the staff Gideon gave him floating on the surface above.

The smell of bacon frying woke Benjamin the next morning.

'Thought you was gonna sleep til next week,' Jeems remarked as he poured himself a cup of coffee.

Sasha stood over the stove, pushing bacon and eggs in two pans. 'Let him be. He was tired. No?'

Benjamin stood bleary-eyed for a few minutes, absorbing the smell of breakfast and the warmth of the house. He knew that it wasn't going to be long lived, as they were due to set out, and by the look of the bags at the door, it was going to be soon.

Taymar sidled up to him on the bench after he sat down. 'Did you have a restful sleep, little warrior?'

'Yeth, thanx,' Benjamin answered, his mouth full of bacon roll.

'Good. We're on the last part of the journey, and you will need your strength.'

'What do you mean?' Benjamin asked her. 'We still have to get back after we get the league.'

'Yeah,' Jeems added. 'I don't want ter have ter escape like the last time. That was close, so it was.'

'But Gideon could come and get us, couldn't he, Taymar?'

She hesitated before nodding slowly. 'He could. But that is not the point, little warrior. The struggle is in the journey and getting the leagues.' Taymar fixed her eyes on Benjamin. 'There is more story yet to be told. There is more to be told on how Meridia got to the state it is in; how men and women-'

'Right, time ter go. Benjermin, get yerself tergether.' Jeems got up from the table, scraping the bench against the floor a little harder than needed. Out of the corner of his eye, Benjamin caught Jeems' steely glare to Taymar. Taymar, for her part, seemed quite unaffected, but continued to eat her breakfast.

It was when Benjamin was coming down the corridor from his room that he overheard Jeems and Taymar talking in her bedroom.

'Ya shouldn't be sayin' all that stuff ter the lad.' Benjamin could see through the crack in the door that Jeems was standing directly opposite Taymar, his hands on his hips. 'He should know. He has a right to know why he has been put in such danger,' Taymar continued stuffing things in to her pack. She glanced up at Jeems, giving Benjamin only seconds to pull himself back.

'That may be so, Taymar, but we both know that yer not the one ter be tellin' him.'

Taymar stopped packing. 'I agree with you, but to watch him,'

'I know wot yer sayin', but we can't interfere.' Jeems paused. 'An' I'm serprised that ya even did wot ya did, so I am.'

Silenced followed and then footsteps towards the bedroom door. Looking around for a place to hide, Benjamin quickly ducked in to an adjacent room before the two walked out and down the corridor. He stayed for a minute, letting his heartbeat get back to normal before he followed them. What was the big secret? And what about Taymar? That was a side to her that he hadn't seen. She really did care about him. And what's with Jeems, anyways? Taymar should be able to tell him everything. All of this secrecy was starting to get to him. He looked around and realised he was in a broom closet. Then, curiously, the words of Gideon came back to him. *'Knowing too much before your time is sometimes worse than not knowing anything at all.'*

He sighed deeply. But wasn't he the one risking his life? His thoughts flashed back to Jeems at the clearing, bound and bloody, to Primrose struggling to fly to the top of Water's Hyde, and to Taymar who single-handedly fought off a group of beasts. It was too much to take sometimes. Then he thought of Will and Jericho, even Hubrice – all of them in hiding and feeling hopeless. It was up to him, he knew that, and so he had to keep going. He stepped out of the closet and caught up to everyone in the front of the house.

Batar had come back in from getting the dogs ready. 'Is cold this morning,' he remarked, icicles hanging from his beard. He turned to Sasha and said something in Russian. She nodded and went to the kitchen, coming back with two hot stones wrapped in many layers of burlap and leather.

'You will want this on you,' Batar handed them to Benjamin as they walked out. The sun was shining brightly, and Benjamin found it difficult to see until Sasha handed him a pair of sunglasses.

'It's so cold,' he commented, his teeth chattering. 'But the sun is shining.'

'Up here, the brighter the sun shines, the colder it is,' Batar said matter-of-factly. 'Here is your sled,' he pointed to the largest one. 'The team is good, it will carry you.'

'I don't have to be carried. It will make me colder if I'm not moving.'

'You know how to drive one do you?' Batar asked. 'I didn't think so. We will be going too fast at the start. Don't worry, you will do plenty of walking,' Batar shook his head and laughed a bit. 'Get in.'

Benjamin felt prickles come up the side of his face. He looked to the house for Sasha, who was watching from the window. 'Is Sasha coming?'

Batar shook his head. 'She stay here and keep track of us,' he showed Benjamin a small pin on the inside of his coat. 'Can go underwater up to 30 meters.' Batar looked around. 'Jeems, you drive this one with the boy.'

Jeems came up, Primrose trailing behind him, shivering. 'Ya'll be fine once ya gets goin'.' Jeems rolled his eyes in Batar's direction.

'Is she alright?' Benjamin asked

'Cold is all.'

'Maybe she wants to stay with Sasha?' Batar asked, wiping icicles away from his mouth.

Primrose nodded eagerly. Jeems looked at the little dragon. 'Yer sure 'bout that? We're goin' a long way, so we are. I can't tell ya when I'll see ya again. It may be awhile.'

Primrose kept nodding.

Jeems twisted his lips, his eyes not leaving Primrose. 'It's just I knows how ya are, so I do. I knows ya'll be pinin' fer me befer long.'

Taymar came up beside Benjamin. 'Or he will be pining for her,' she said in his ear, causing them both to smile.

Benjamin guessed Jeems must have caught this exchange, because he gave an irritated shrug and said. 'Awright, then, but ya've got ter promise ter be on yer best behaviour, so ya do. And don't be givin' Sasha no trouble. She'll have enough ter be worryin' about, so she will.'

Primrose nodded quickly, and leapt for joy. Without waiting to say goodbye, she bounded back towards the research station.

Jeems watched her leave. 'Chicken,' he said, shaking his head.

'You made her soft,' Batar joked. 'Treating her so nice. She is dragon, no? You teach her to be fierce and fearless, not soft and nervous.'

'Keep talkin' Batar,' Jeems quipped. 'I'm not the one who tried ter keep a killer whale as a pet. That's my personal favourite, so it is.'

Benjamin and Taymar exchanged looks, eyebrows raised. Batar merely shrugged. 'Was worth a try. Is good to have a killer whale on your side, no?'

'As long as he's on yer side an' not tryin' ter take off the left side o' yer body,' Jeems shot back.

Batar continued laughing while Benjamin struggled to get himself on the sled. The weight and thickness of his coat made it difficult to bend in to a sitting position. His face grew hot as he wiggled and twisted.

'Comfy?' Jeems asked after a few moments. Benjamin picked up the sarcasm in his voice.

'Just – a – I – can't – get - - uh – there.' Benjamin sighed deeply and settled in, facing out towards endless ice and snow.

With a shout from Batar, all three sleds set off. The dogs were well rested and, with Batar's team leading, were going faster than the previous night. The spray from Batar's sled covered Benjamin's entire face, and he was secretly happy that Sasha had insisted he wear a pair of snow goggles over his balaclava.

They carried on for two days, only stopping for a few hours to eat, sleep and let the dogs rest. Benjamin rode most of the way, but when he knew the dogs were getting tired, he would try and run beside the sled. This would work for a while, but then he would fall, and Taymar or Jeems would have to help him up because of all the layers he had on.

He never remembered having to work so hard in his life. It made him think of all the times him and Marcus would run away from Motley. Even then he never felt this tired or ran this far. He thought about Will and how things must be for him at the minute. He hoped that Will was able to escape the night of the fire. Nothing would be worse down there than having Hubrice angry him. Finally, on the third day of travelling they came to what looked like huge chunks of snow piled on top of each other.

'You will have to walk from here,' Batar turned to Benjamin.

'Where are we?' he asked, scrambling to get up, like a tortoise on its back.

Nobody answered and Benjamin soon realised why. Once he took off his goggles, he saw the open space of hard packed snow with a mixture of cracks and mounds of ice. Huge chunks of ice, piled on top of each other, stood randomly as far as they could see. In their shadow lay cracks in the ground, like jagged black lines in the snow.

'Crags and crevassees,' Batar said from behind Benjamin. He stretched his hand out over Benjamin's shoulder. 'Sometimes crevassees go for miles. Crags look solid but can shift and come down on you without warning.'

'So the crags are those piles of ice and the crevassees are those little cracks.'

Batar nodded. 'But don't be fooled. They look like little cracks, but one bad move and they can open up wide enough for you to fall in.'

'To where?'

Batar shrugged. 'Does it matter? The point is you'd never be seen again.'

Benjamin scanned the tundra with a nervous eye. 'Can't we just walk around it?'

Batar shook his head. 'There is no way to tell where the crevassees start and where they end. Some crevassees are hidden few inches under the snow,' he stamped his feet, making Benjamin tense. 'Only when you walk over one do you know it is there, and by then it's too late.'

'So how do we,' Benjamin trailed off.

'You guessed it,' Batar grinned. 'We walk through it.'

'How?'

'Very carefully.' His tone took on a serious note. 'And we need to start, days are not long up here.'

It looked innocent enough, Benjamin thought to himself as he helped unharness the dogs. It was dead quiet except for the dogs' anxious whimpers, and he was starting to convince himself that nothing would happen at all. Then as if out of thin air, something Gideon had once said came to his mind. *Sometimes it's what looks innocent that proves to be the most deadly.*

Three dogs brushed past Benjamin as they all roamed free, patting and sniffing the hard snow. Taymar and Batar walked by, pulling the sleds with harnesses strapped around their waist.

'The dogs're better goin' across on their own,' Jeems explained. 'You 'n me'll go across tergether. It's a good thing Primrose stayed back, so it is. She'd 've never made it across this minefield. Here,' Jeems pushed an end of Benjamin's rope in to his hand. 'Tie this end around yer waist.'

Benjamin did as he was told. 'And if I fall?'

'Then I'm comin' with ya, ain't I?' Jeems winked, pointing to the rope around his waist. 'But

234

here's hopin' that won't happen. Just stay close an' follow me. Ya'll be awright.'

They all set off across the landscape, Benjamin on Jeems' heels behind Taymar, then Batar who was leading the way. Time passed slowly. No one dared talk for fear that the sound waves would cause the crags to shift.

Then a yelp to the right. Benjamin could just see the top half of a dog clawing at the packed snow, its bottom half fallen through a crevasse. He made a move to help, but was stopped by Jeems.

'Batar'll get her. Just her struggling will cause the crevasse to widen.' As Jeems spoke a crack ripped through the air and the crevasse stretched towards them. Snow, once lightly covering the gap, fell in to it as it widened and advanced, gaining speed.

'Benjermin, we gotta get away from that crevasse,' he could hear Jeems' voice, but seemed glued to the spot.

'C'mon Benjermin. Move!'

It got closer, the rumbling sound chasing it. He realised how cold his feet were, sunk up to his ankles in snow.

'Come on!' Jeems yanked on the rope, pulling Benjamin off his feet. He felt the snow give way as his feet left the ground. He landed face down in the snow, inches away from the icy cavern that had now separated the travellers from the research station. The rumbling and cracking continued until it was out of earshot.

Jeems lay panting on the ground beside him. 'I'm sorry Jeems. I guess I just panicked.'

Jeems gave a quick nod. 'Ya've seen fer yerself now, so ya have, how quick they come about.'

Batar came striding over, a worn look on his face. The crag towering over him creaked.

'We've lost one dog,' he announced as Taymar joined them.

Benjamin's head bowed under the weight of what he had just heard. 'What do we do now?' His tongue felt thick.

'We wait,' Batar answered solemly. He whistled to gather the dogs, one eye on the crag behind them.

'Here?' Benjamin caught Jeems' eye.

'That crevasse may still be goin'. If we're lucky, it won't set anything else off. But most o' the time once one goes ya can be sure another one'll be close behind, so it will.'

Batar nodded. 'And I don't like how that crag looks.' He pointed to the mound of ice behind him. 'We should move away. We keep close to the crevasse and we'll be okay.'

Taymar and Jeems agreed, and they set out, dogs in tow. Benjamin turned once more to look at the crag, and was shocked to see that the crag's shadow had changed shape.

'Jeems,' Benjamin trotted up to him. 'I think there's something behind that crag.'

'Eh?'

'The crag. When I turned back to look at it, the shadow changed.'

Their eyes met. 'It's nothin',' Jeems said after a pause. 'Just the sun changing position.'

As they got further away from the crag, Benjamin noticed Taymar's suspicious backwards glances.

They travelled far. Benjamin's knees were starting to buckle, and his snowshoes were getting heavier and heavier. Dusk was turning in to night, but it was impossible to know the time of day. Batar had warned them that it never really got light in the winter. The dreary weather crept in to their souls.

'You mean you wish to keep going?' Taymar's voice seemed far away. Benjamin stopped and stretched his neck around his hood. About twenty feet behind him they stopped to make camp and he hadn't even noticed.

Jeems met him halfway. 'You awright?'

He nodded stiffly.

'Ya sure? Is summat wrong? Are ya hurt?'

'No, nothing like that. Was just thinking about everything and –'

Jeems nodded his head encouragingly.

Benjamin looked at him. 'Well, and how we're going to get there. I can't believe we lost a dog. Poor Batar, he must be really upset.'

Jeems patted Benjamin's shoulder and looked over to where Batar was unpacking one of the sleds. 'Batar's had ter deal with way worse. No doubt he's a little upset, but, he knows wot we're doin' out 'ere is important, so he does.' Their eyes met. 'There's summat about this 'ere environment that gets people down, so there is. Try ter focus on wot ya have done, and how far ya have got. Leave the worries of how yer gonna get there ter us lot. We've taken ya this far.'

'I know, I know,' Benjamin started forward. 'Thanks Jeems.'

'Don't mention it, mate.'

Between the four of them, setting up camp went really fast. Benjamin helped Taymar with the fire and was amazed at how fast Batar and Jeems made two igloos. Batar was like a machine, cutting blocks of hard snow with his huge machete. Jeems kept up with him, stacking the blocks as fast as they were cut.

'Jeems knows how to do everything,' Benjamin said to Taymar.

Taymar stopped stoking the fire and looked up. 'Yes, he is very skilled. He's warm and courageous too, but he doesn't believe it and it eats through him.'

Benjamin knew what she was talking about. 'I think people can change.'

'I agree with you, little warrior,' Taymar started cooking with an old iron pot nestled in the fire. 'And our friend Jeems is one example of that. The most difficult part about changing is believing you have. Since Howl, Meridia has always been divided in to those who follow Gideon and those who do not. Magh was created as a diversion really, a tactic to make people believe what they were doing wasn't that bad. But at the end of it, it's black and white; good and evil.

239

And just as there have been those who have gone from following Gideon to following Magh, so are there ones like Jeems who have turned from Magh and have chosen to give their lives to what Gideon is trying to achieve for Meridia.'

'I don't understand why he doesn't think he's good now.'

Taymar shook her head slightly. 'Because you humans are strange creatures. Even when you follow Gideon, you still let doubt creep in. Jeems doesn't think he is good enough to be loved, and so that leaves a little opening for lies to grow in his head that he's worthless, nothing and that he'll never change. It's up to you to believe it or not. Gideon can only do so much for you and then you have to choose.'

Eating dinner around the fire they planned which way they were going to go in the morning. To his surprise, Benjamin joined in and even made suggestions. It was a good sign, Jeems had said, because it meant he was growing up. Taymar commented that it must mean he was becoming more responsible for his journey, but Benjamin wasn't sure how much more responsible he could be, risking his life and all. He made sure to say the last part under his breath and when no one was looking. He tried not to roll his eyes, but couldn't help it, and it was then that he caught what looked like streaks of rainbows dancing in the night sky. He gazed at them, unable to take his eyes off the thick ribbons of colour weaving through the stars.

'You like?' Batar asked.

'They're beautiful. Totally amazing.'

'Northern Lights. Well, they have different names wherever you go. Sasha's people call them fire foxes, the Bogwumps call them something I can't pronounce. Sasha's grandfather used to say that if you whistled at them, they would come down to either help or hurt you.'

'How d'ya know which they'd do?' Jeems asked.

'You don't. Some believe that they are sentaphs dancing across the sky, and they will help the good but hurt those that seek to do evil.'

'Sounds like something I'd like on my side,' Benjamin laughed.

'Why you joke?' Batar cocked his head. 'You don't believe what I say?'

'I don't know. Sounds strange.'

'Strange, maybe. But good in a fight if they like you.' Batar headed in to the igloo. 'Goodnight everyone.'

'Are the dogs secure?' Taymar asked.

Jeems nodded. 'Put 'em in the other igloo meself, so I did. Yer sure worried 'bout them, ain't ya.'

'I'm not convinced the dog caused that crevasse to split,' she answered.

With Taymar's last comment hanging heavy in the air, they all crawled in to the igloo and settled in. Benjamin was exhausted, and didn't have much trouble getting to sleep, restless as it was. He shifted uncomfortably on the hard snow, moving in and out of dreams ranging from unpleasant to terrifying. His dreams found him back at Hadley Priest, watching an exchange between Marcus and Motley, to Hester who by now was frantic with Benjamin's second disappearance, convinced that she was going to lose her job. But it was the last dream that stirred him awake, one of him standing atop a mountain looking down on the ocean, face to face with an enormous sea creature.

He didn't know how long the dogs had been whining by the time he woke up but guessed it couldn't have been long because everyone else was fast asleep. He lay there for a minute, listening to their low whimpers, only getting up to investigate when they started to get louder.

He crawled out of the igloo, thinking that all he needed to do was set them straight as they were probably getting on top of each other. However as he poked his head out he saw a huge wolf-like animal trying to get to the dogs.

'Ah! Jeems! Hey, there's a wolf thing trying to get to the dogs!'

Taymar was first up, pulling Benjamin back in by his ankles. She swept past him with Batar close behind, leaving Jeems struggling with his boots.

'Stupid thing,' he said under his breath, hopping on one leg. Before long he had bounded out as well adding a stern 'stay 'ere.'

Benjamin listened to the commotion outside; a mixture of wolf growls and hollers. From the opaque walls of the igloo Benjamin could see flames as they tried to scare the beasts away. The snarling and growling got louder, deeper and seemed to multiply. As anxious as he was getting, it was the painful cry from Jeems that got him outside.

As he scrambled out he saw six huge wolves around his three friends. Grey in colour and much bigger than any wolf he had seen in photos, their lower jaw stuck out further than their top one, giving them a fiercer look.

Jeems cried out again to Benjamin's left, struggling with a particularly big wolf. Almost a third bigger than the others, the wolf had Jeems pinned to the ground, its mouth around his throat. Three times Benjamin tried to shout for Taymar or Batar but his voice never came. He groped around in the dark, trying to find something he could use to help Jeems. Then the fire flickered and he saw his staff off to the side tied to one of the sleds. He darted across the snow and fumbled to untie it, heading back to Jeems when it was finally free.

Benjamin didn't realise he was yelling until the wolf turned to look at him, and then a few things happened all at once. He had just started to swing his staff when he sank up to his hips in the snow. In one leap the wolf was virtually on top of him with Benjamin barely having enough time to hold his staff up in front of him.

The wolf gripped the staff in his mouth, his jaws locked on it. It thrashed Benjamin's upper body about, unable to dislodge him from the snow. He hung on to the staff tightly with both hands, his arms shoulder-width apart, hoping the beast would soon get tired. His back muscles started to burn and he knew that in a few moments his arms would give way. Out of the corner of his eye he saw Taymar striding towards where Jeems lay, perched on his elbow, bleeding from his chest.

'Taymar,' Benjamin gasped. Looking towards him, she strode over, her sword in her hand. With one swipe the wolf crumpled to the ground next to them, the staff falling out of its mouth.

'Are you alright, little warrior?' Taymar asked in a hurried voice.

Benjamin nodded. 'Is Jeems okay?'

She nodded. 'He'll be fine, it is only a flesh wound.' She pointed towards the two wolves that were left. 'Look, they are leaving.'

Benjamin watched as the wolves ran in to the night, yelping and howling. He struggled to get out of his snowy trap.

'Save your strength,' Taymar gently held his shoulder. 'Batar will come and dig you out in a minute.' She strode back to Jeems and started wrapping his wounds.

Batar trotted over with a shovel. 'Now you know why snowshoes good, yes?'

'Yeh,' Benjamin said in a shaky voice. 'I guess I wasn't thinking.'

Batar grunted playfully and slowly started to shift the snow. When he had dug down to Benjamin's knees he pulled him out. 'We must leave soon. We cannot wait until morning. Brush snow off so you are not cold. In fact, start packing up. That will keep you warm.' He tossed a pair of snowshoes down and went over to Taymar and Jeems. Jeems waved feebly to Benjamin who waved back before struggling to put his snowshoes on. Once they were on, he picked up his staff and crawled back in to the igloo to pack things up.

He had gotten all of the bedrolls done up and most everything else stacked neatly outside the igloo when Taymar came up behind him.

'Well done, little warrior.'

'There wasn't much stuff out,' Benjamin looked around. 'I was just going to start loading it on the sled.'

'I meant about how you helped Jeems. Are you alright?'

Benjamin tied and untied his bedroll twice. 'I guess so. Yeah.'

'That was a very brave thing you did.'

Benjamin crawled outside and piled two cooking pots on the sled. 'Is he hurt real bad?'

Taymar followed him. 'A gash on his chest. It could have been much worse. I suspect it was a warning more than anything.'

They looked at each other. 'It's a good thing you made Batar and Jeems build that igloo for the dogs,' Benjamin finally broke the silence.

'Yes, I guess we both saved some lives tonight. I'll take these,' she left with two sleeping rolls under her arms.

'Taymar, do you remember when I said that crag before had a strange shadow?'

'I do indeed.'

'I kept getting the feeling that something was behind it.'

Taymar nodded. 'You have become very sensitive to the forces at work in Meridia, little warrior. I felt the same way. I am sure that we were being followed, and that is the reason behind this attack.'

'Wow, I'm getting good at something I'm not sure I want to be good at,' Benjamin responded.

'On the contrary, it will help you no end while you continue your journey. Now let's get moving.'

Benjamin crawled back in to the igloo to make sure he hadn't forgotten anything.

'There ya are,' Jeems called out to Benjamin as he crawled out of the igloo feet first.

'Are you alright?' Benjamin stumbled to his feet. 'Stupid snowshoes.'

'I'll be fine.' Jeems hesitated. 'Wot made ya wake up anyways? Did ya hear the dogs?'

'I had a bad dream. Well, more like dreams.'

'Anything ya need ter talk 'bout?' Jeems studied Benjamin's face.

'Nah, they were all really random.'

'If yer sure.' Jeems paused. 'I s'pose I owe ya me thanks again.'

'All I did was get stuck in the snow,' Benjamin shrugged. 'It's not like I went up against a rock monster or distracted a giant for you.'

They exchanged a smile. 'Darn cold weather,' Jeems blinked and pressed his finger in to his eye.

'Yeah,' Benjamin sniffed.

16

Water and Ice

The dogs, jittery and anxious from their scare with the wolves, did not need much encouragement to get going. Jeems insisted that he run alongside them, but they ran so fast that he struggled to keep up. A tight bandage around his torso, he stumbled across the snow trying to stay beside the sled. It wasn't long before he fell behind, and it took a stern word from Batar to get him to ride along. Grunting and mumbling, he finally gave in, all the while insisting that he was fine.

'Of course you are fine, but also you are slow. I don't want to be wolf dinner.' Batar strapped Jeems on to the sled. 'The dogs run fast right now, they are still scared. Is good.'

Taymar and Benjamin exchanged smiles before they set off again. They continued on through the night, following the crevasse that had claimed the life of Batar's dog, Shu. The darkness was thick, making it difficult to see. As they went on, the Northern Lights floated down and lighted their path, the hues of colour swirling above their heads. The crevasse curved to the right, leading them in the direction of the league while bursts of shimmery colour filled the sky as the lights danced and dove down towards the ground.

Exhausted, Benjamin hopped onto his sled sometime in to the night and slipped in and out of sleep. He woke hours later, feeling a fresh dampness in the air, his nose ice cold.

Jeems guided their sled next to Batar and Taymar who had stopped just before the coastline. On the shore looking out on to the narrow bay, the ocean stretched out far and wide. Beyond the bay icebergs rose majestically out of the water. Strange noises off to the left where orcas were hunting seals.

'That is good,' Batar pointed to the hungry orcas. 'That means Sqwal is nowhere around. For now.' He scanned the coastline until his eyes stopped to the far right. 'There,' he pointed to a particularly big iceberg. 'Pressed up against the rocks. That is where we are going.'

It was difficult to see at first, due to the distance. Batar led Benjamin with his finger, along the rocky ledge of the bay. At the edge of the cliff, where the bay widened to open water, sat their target.

'Yeah, I see it, but it looks like all the rest.' Benjamin shaded his eyes with his hands before routing around for the sunglasses Sasha had packed him.

'Well, ya don't want it lookin' different, do ya?' Jeems came up, empty dog halters in his hands. 'Might as well leave the league out in the open then.' He shared a grin with Batar.

The air was crisp, and even the sun struggled to burn through the winter sky. The sound of sea birds played in the background as water pushed up against the rocky cliff off to the right. Atop the cliff was a flat surface that jutted right out to the end of the bay. Just before the iceberg they were after, the cliff's side sloped down towards the water. It looked as though snow had run down that part of the cliff on numerous occasions, because unlike the rest of the rocky wall it was packed down like a ski run.

Benjamin sighed, trying to sound as if he wasn't bothered by the killer whales so close by. 'I guess now all we have to do is?'

'Is wait,' Batar interrupted.

Benjamin looked at him.

'Those orcas are hungry! Look at them!' Batar exclaimed, pointing to the pod that had gotten closer. 'I don't want to be orca lunch. Sqwal is bad enough, but now you send me in water with orcas! No way. We will wait until they leave, then we will go.'

'Sounds good to me,' Benjamin announced. He turned and automatically started helping Jeems unpack some breakfast.

Taymar, who had gone off to scout the area had come back. She looked windblown, her cheeks rosy.

'Awright?' Jeems asked.

'I've seen nothing to alert us,' Taymar answered. She motioned her head towards the pod of orcas. 'We'll have to wait for them to move on.'

Jeems pushed a mouthful of food to his cheek. 'It'll be awhile. They like to play wif there food 'fore eatin'.'

Benjamin stopped chewing and looked at Jeems.

'What?'

'That was gross.' He tossed the rest of his roll on the ice.

'Whadda ya mean?'

'I really don't need to be reminded that I could become whale food at any moment,' Benjamin huffed.

'Yer not gonna become whale food,' Jeems replied, moving his head from side to side with every word. 'We'll wait til they're gone. Ya might be summat's dinner, but not those whales.' He chuckled. Benjamin looked away.

'I'm only messin' around with ya, so I am.'

'Humph.' Benjamin looked at his breakfast lying in the snow. Even though he was colder than he ever was at Hadley Priest, he had never gone hungry here. And although he had never been as scared before, living back at Hadley Priest still seemed harder than getting the leagues. The thought of ever going back brought a lump to his throat.

'We will have to watch him much closer than before.' Taymar's voice unwittingly carried across to Benjamin. Out of the corner of his eye he could see her talking to Jeems off to the side. He bent his head down lower, trying to regain interest in his breakfast.

Jeems kept looking ahead and chewing, his head nodding slowly.

'I am unsure how much longer we will be one step ahead of them,' Taymar continued. 'And from what I have heard, it has gotten difficult for his friends on the other side of the door.'

Benjamin darted his eyes away from Taymar as she glanced towards him.

'I imagine Gideon would wish to keep the boy here from now on. It would be easier if he were to stay in Meridia, things would get done quicker, would you not agree?'

Jeems kept chewing while casting a look over to Benjamin. 'I've got no idea wot Gideon's plans are, so I don't. I s'pose we'll have ter wait an' see.'

Out of the corner of his eye, Benjamin could see Jeems looking at him. He picked up his roll and nibbled at it. The thought of not having to go back to Hadley Priest sent a tingling sensation down his spine, mixed with sadness at the thought of not seeing Marcus and Riley. Then forgotten anger and confusion returned. Why hadn't Marcus told him the truth? The coded note said it all, Marcus had always known about Meridia. The only friends he seemed to have left were here – Jeems, Will. Even Taymar and Batar were more trustworthy than anyone on the other side of the cellar door.

'I say we sleep,' Batar had come back from feeding the dogs. 'We can go in research hut.' He pointed off to the left, where a small building sat close to the shoreline.

They packed up quickly, Benjamin keeping one eye on the orcas that were slowly making their way to open sea. By the time they had got in to the building and settled in, he was so tired he could barely see straight. After getting his bedroll out, he fell asleep, listening to the sound of the ice floes jamming against each other.

17

Sqwal

'Ya want summat ter eat?'

The question seemed far away. Then a poke in the shoulder.

'Wake up, ya've bin sleepin' fer four hours,' Jeems' voice filtered through sleep.

Disoriented, Benjamin looked around.

He hadn't really paid attention to the research shack before he fell asleep, he was that tired. But now, he gained interest. The hut, just big enough for them and their stuff had a simple wooden desk and filing cabinet that took up the remaining floor space. There was a camp bed in the corner with Batar's bedroll on it and an over-used pillow. The white walls were bare, save for a technical looking map of the area that was pinned up above the desk. Smaller versions of the equipment at Batar's house were piled atop the desk and filing cabinet, hidden under dust covers.

'Do ya want summat ter eat?' Jeems asked again. 'I'm makin' sandwiches.' Jeems had claimed a small space of the desk to make sandwiches with various fillings.

Benjamin yawned. 'What time is it?'

'Early afternoon, I'd say. But this'll be the last time I ask ya, do ya want a sandwich?'

'Er – yeah. Anything but that salmon mush. That stuff's gross.' Benjamin started packing up his bedroll.

'Oi!' Jeems responded. 'I love that stuff, so I do.' He slapped a mound of it on a piece of bread. 'Whadda ya think, Taymar? In't it the best sandwich filling ya've ever tasted?'

'I think that if it was the only sandwich filling left to survive on,' she plugged her nose. 'Then you could live on bread alone.'

Benjamin chuckled.

'Aw, wot d'ya know?' Jeems chortled.

Batar came in, the thick mist of cold air rising up behind him.

'Is cold, very cold,' he announced as he shut the door behind him. Small icicles hung from his moustache and beard, moving up and down as he spoke. 'Dogs will need to come inside when we leave.'

'Batar, how are we going to get to that iceberg?' Benjamin asked as Jeems passed him a sandwich.

'I have boat under research hut. The motor was cold, did not want to start, but I fixed it.'

'There ya are, ol' friend,' Jeems passed him a sandwich. 'Salmon pate.'

'Ah! My favourite. Cheers, as you say.' Batar and Jeems gestured towards each other before taking a bite of their sandwiches. Taymar pretended to gag, making Benjamin snort.

Jeems savoured his mouthful, gazing down at his sandwich. 'There's summat special 'bout this 'ere pate,' he said thoughtfully.

'My Sasha made it,' Batar responded proudly.

'Well, there's that an' all. But, there's summat else, so there is. There's an extra ingredient in there,' he smacked his lips together. 'Summat's in 'ere that makes it taste better than any other I've ever had.'

'Ah, I know what you mean.' Batar nodded.

'Ya do?'

'Yes. Special ingredient.'

'Yeh. Wot is it?'

'Salmon eyes.'

Taymar spat her drink out at the same time as Jeems dropped the rest of his sandwich. 'Wha-' was all Jeems could manage.

'Eyes are good for filler,' Batar explained. 'Sasha soaks them first then squeezes-'

Batar's words were drowned by the sounds of Jeems groaning and Taymar and Benjamin laughing.

It was early afternoon by the time they had pulled themselves together and packed up. Jeems had rinsed his mouth out twice while Batar looked on, a puzzled expression on his face. The winter sun was low when they reached the shore, but the water was calm and quiet.

'Maybe we should wait 'til mornin' now,' suggested Jeems, looking up at the sky.

Batar shrugged. 'You wait, orcas might come back. Is winter. Animals always hunt in the day. Sun never gets too bright.'

'It is not wise to linger,' Taymar added. 'As long as our little warrior-'

'Why do you call me that?' Benjamin interrupted.

'Because you are a warrior,' Taymar answered.

'But so is everyone else here.'

'They know what the other choice is,' Taymar replied. 'They have seen the consequences of following Magh. But you, you have not seen it and yet you choose to stay and fight. You could leave Meridia and forget this place even exists, but you don't. You stay and you fight. Not for you but for others. That makes you a true warrior.'

There was silence for a few moments. Benjamin didn't know where to look. The cold bit his nose and cheeks. 'I'm freezing,' he finally managed through chattering teeth.

'Taymar's right, ya are a warrior. An' yer right an' all, it's freezin' out here so let's get this done so we can get back in the warm.'

After making sure the dogs were inside and safe, they dragged the huge inflatable raft along the shore, dipping it gently in to the water, skimming along the large, flat stones. Feet splashed in the shallow sea.

'Okay, get in,' Batar said once they were ankle deep. Benjamin and Jeems climbed in while Taymar and Batar pushed out a bit further before jumping in themselves.

They sat on the inflatable seats that ran the width of the boat in three rows, drifting for a few minutes while Batar fiddled with the motor. Tiny ice crystals hung in the air, as dusk approached. They clung to Benjamin's eyelashes, making him cross-eyed. After a few pulls on the rip wire, the motor sputtered to life and they headed out.

As big as the icebergs were from the shore, they were twice the size close up. They towered overhead as Batar manoeuvred through them. It was like going through a minefield, as the base of the icebergs ran deep and wide under the water.

Benjamin looked up, icebergs surrounding them. The cold air made his eyes water and his nose run.

As they came out of the bay towards open sea the water got choppy, causing the little boat to bob under the waves. 'It's close,' Batar shouted over the buzz of the motor, pointing to the right. Running parallel to them was the cliff that jetted out towards the iceberg they were heading to. It sat directly below the point of the cliff, jammed up against the rocky edge. The waves crashed against it, and Benjamin couldn't see how he was going to get in. The side of the cliff, mostly rocky and steep, softened as it reached the point. Covered in snow, the cliff side looked dangerous, with piles of overblown snow piled high on top of each other.

Batar slowed the motor as they crept along towards the back of the iceberg. Benjamin felt for his staff and rope, making sure they were securely tied to his belt. It wasn't until they were almost right against the cliff that Benjamin saw the slim gap between it and the iceberg, just below the water's surface.

'You have wetsuit under those clothes?' Batar asked Benjamin.

He nodded, fumbling with the buttons on his jacket, his hands trembling.

Jeems leant over to help him. 'Did ya ever learn that breathing technique from Sasha?'

'Er-' Benjamin dodged Jeems' glare.

'It's no good strappin' an oxygen tank on yer back, ya'd never make it through that little opening, so you won't.'

'Sasha said I got the basics,' he answered through chattering teeth.

'Well, from what I understand, the opening in't that far underwater. Ya'll be fine,' Jeems smiled reassuringly. 'I'll come in the water with ya, just wait 'til I get my coat off.'

Jeems got ready while Batar used the motor to fight against the current. Taymar hung out the front, pushing off the cliff every time they got too close.

'Remember, depending on tide, the opening could be quite deep' Batar said, his voice raised over the wind and the waves. 'And another thing-'

Batar was interrupted when a fierce crack rumbled through the air. It echoed across the water, causing icebergs to tremble. They looked to the cliff where the sound had come from. Directly above them a huge chunk of snow had broken off and was tumbling down the snowy side.

'It's comin' down fast,' Jeems shouted. 'Get us outta here, Batar.'

The low rumbling got louder as the avalanche gained momentum, bringing more snow with it as it hurtled towards the little boat.

'Batar!' Taymar jumped over Benjamin to where the researcher was fiddling with the motor as it coughed out.

Benjamin held on to the sides of the boat as Taymar brushed past him. 'Here!' She thrust an oar in his face. 'We need to get out of its path.'

Jeems and Benjamin paddled against the waves while Taymar and Batar tried to fix the motor.

Thoughts sped through Benjamin's mind. They needed to hurry up. They needed to hide, but there was nowhere to go.

'Get down!' It was the last thing Benjamin heard before the snow hit. The force hurtled him out of the boat and in to the icy water. Piles of snow tumbled in after him, driving him further down. He forced his eyes open, the salt stinging them. To his right was the wall of an iceberg. His hand shot out towards it. Sharp ice and then a twinge of pain in his hand as blood coloured the water red. Recovering, he found an icy ridge to cling to, letting the piles of snow sink passed him.

The current swirled around as he swam back to the surface. It hugged his body, rushing through his pockets. Then over him, flipping him upside down. Struggling, the piece of sea glass that Jericho gave him dislodged from his pocket and sank out of his reach. He watched it go down, relieved it wasn't the stone with the oracle on it. Just before it was out of sight, it started to glow bright green. Fighting against his need to breathe, he watched it swell and glow brighter until it exploded in to a million tiny particles. The sound followed. The enormous, thunderous boom that came from the explosion of that small piece of glass cracked icebergs in half. The waves it caused forced Benjamin upwards.

He broke surface and took a desperate gasp of air. The waves were ferocious, making it difficult to see. Rising up, he saw Jeems clutching to the raft, swimming towards Batar who was floating on top of the water.

'Jeems!' He called out.

'Over here,' Taymar's voice made him turn around. A few strokes and he was in her arms.

'We must get to shore!' Taymar shouted. 'The explosion has woken Sqwal.'

'Taymar,' Benjamin was confused. 'The explosion -'

'It sounded like a piece of sea glass. They were created by Magh to wake the deepest beasts of the ocean. She would use them to summon sea creatures to overtake fishermen when they were at sea.'

Memories rushed at Benjamin. The piece of glass. Jericho. He insisted Benjamin take it. The dream of the snakes, how they twisted around each other. Twist. Jericho Twist.

'Taymar! I know who the traitor is. I know-'

The shriek that came from the depths of the ocean was ear splitting. Wincing, they covered their ears as Jeems came towards them with the raft.

'Swim!' Jeems called out. When Taymar and Benjamin got to the raft, Batar was already in, slumped across the seats.

'Is he?' Benjamin couldn't say the words.

'He's alive, just knocked out,' Jeems answered. 'Hurry up! Sqwal's comin', so it is.'

They scrambled in to the raft, swollen waves crashing in to it, thrashing it against the icebergs. Jeems and Taymar paddled desperately to shore while Benjamin scanned the surface of the water. And then behind them the blue water turned black. A shadow, a patch of darkness was coming towards them.

'Jeems.' About 50 meters away he could see the shadow growing, its heaviness lifting out of the deep water.

It was the creatures' tail that Benjamin saw first. With an almighty whoosh it came out of the water, only meters away from them. The tail alone was as wide as a house was high, and almost as thick as his mattress at Hadley Priest. As it raised up, water poured from it, showering the miniature raft beneath it. They looked up at it towering above them. On its way down, the

265

wind that was generated pushed the boat back. It hit the water hard and fast. Too fast. None of them had time to act. Water engulfed them, and once again they were thrown.

Benjamin hit his back against the side of an iceberg and slid down. Without warning he plunged back in to the icy water, salty bubbles swirling around his face. He bobbed back to the surface, hollering and searching for the others.

Between the swells he could see his three friends, thrown like rag dolls across the ruthless icebergs. Jeems had landed on an iceberg and was crawling towards Batar, who was again floating face down in the water beside the raft. Taymar. Where was Taymar?

'You are at the league, little warrior!' He heard her voice. 'You are where you need to be.' He twisted around in the water, looking up to where he thought the voice was coming from.

It was then that he realised he was against the cliff, nestled in to the back of the iceberg. He kept looking up, hoping to see Taymar's long black hair, convincing himself she was still alive and that he had heard her voice.

Taymar didn't disappoint. On the side of the cliff above him to his right, on a low-lying ledge covered in snow she stood, waving to him, motioning with her hand to keep going. 'You must hurry. Sqwal will try and stop you!'

Benjamin nodded numbly, chancing another quick glance to Jeems and Batar before going under. Sqwal was there, smashing through an iceberg to get to Batar, who was still floating face down in the water. Jeems, desperately trying to get to him without sliding in himself was only using one arm, the other, obviously broken, flopping at his side.

Taymar again. 'Go now, I will find a way to Jeems.'

Another dumb nod and with a deep breath, Benjamin went under to look for the opening. The salt water attacked his eyes again, but it was much clearer in this shallow part. He followed the iceberg down, resisting his body's natural urge to float to the surface. Behind him, not far away he could hear Sqwal shriek and groan, crashing through the ice to get to Batar. Benjamin pushed the thought out of his mind as he gropped for the opening.

He didn't have to go down far. It was towards the back, almost jammed up against the cliff that continued down for miles. Just like the diary that Batar had back at his house, the way in was covered by a thick sheet of ice. Benjamin pressed his nose against the clear sheet of frozen water. He could see small stairs, carved out of ice, leading up and in to the middle of the iceberg, twisting out of sight. He looked around, banging his hands against the cold impenetrable door. Even with the breathing Sasha taught him, he was going to have to go back up for air if he didn't figure out how to get through the door. He twisted around, his staff getting jammed between the two hard surfaces. The idea came to him as he was wrestling to free it. With enough strength left for at least one good try, he untied his staff, steadied himself against the cliff and hit the door with everything he had. A dull crack sounded and the door fell apart in three chunks.

Pushing himself off the cliff with his feet, he swam through the opening towards the stairs. By the time he reached the first step, fresh ice had grown over the opening once again, stopping any more water from coming in. He sat shivering, his chest heaving in and out, his wet hair turning to icicles. Frozen fingers secured his staff back against him. I've got to keep going or I'm going to freeze, was his overriding thought. It was the thought he chose, because the ones of Batar and Jeems paralyzed him. He turned to the stairs. Wet and slippery, they were as lethal as they looked. After sliding down twice, he managed to get in to a pattern of inching his way up on his hands and knees. On the third stair he stopped. Something was wrong. He could feel it. He turned to look down at the opening, shut tight. And then he felt it.

Wham! The impact sent him flying back down to the small pool of water at the bottom of the stairs. Another hit followed by a groan and that now familiar shriek. Sqwal had found him. He started up the stairs, inching his way towards the top, clinging to the sides and digging his staff in to the stairs as much as possible to steady himself.

Wham. Wham. Then cracking. Reaching the top stair, Benjamin looked around, expecting to find a hole where Sqwal had broke through, but there was none. He looked ahead to the league.

'Yes!' He shouted. A few feet in front of him in a bowl made of ice a small stream of water swirled around. The bowl was cold, despite blue flame that flickered under it.

On all fours he inched towards it, slipping every so often, his leg or arm extending to the point where his face would hit the ice floor. Then, his wet glove wrapped itself around the bowl and he was staring down in to it. The swirling water, like liquid crystal, the light blue flame underneath, keeping it warm.

He struggled out of his wet gloves. Wham! Another hit followed by a deep crack and then movement. Sqwal had dislodged the iceberg and was pushing it out to open water. Benjamin struggled with the Arcrux, his fingers white and numb with cold. He got the chamber open and dipped the Arcrux in to the swirling water. In moments the chamber was full and as he clicked it shut the water disappeared and the flame went out. Fastening his staff back to his belt he headed back towards the stairs, but was thrown down them as Sqwal rammed the iceberg. He sank in the pool of water below, the door smashed open with water rushing in. His arms burned as he struggled to get out against the rushing water. His hands found the sides and he pulled himself through and out to open water.

There was no telling how far out Sqwal had taken him. To his left he could barely make out the cliff in the distance. He was almost to the surface when the sound came. A shriek and then a groan. He twisted around to face it. The creature no one had ever gotten close to and survived – Sqwal.

The moments seemed like hours as he looked at the beast, both of them suspended in the ocean a few feet from the surface. Metres away the beasts' many eyes fixed on him. Its scales ugly against the night sky.

What's it going to do? It must be trying to drown me. He couldn't stay under any longer. Quickly he paddled upwards, reaching the surface only to be dragged down again by its two huge tentacles. Protruding from its belly, the tentacles brought Benjamin closer. Despite having a wide mouth filled with teeth, there was another along its underside. Surrounded by tentacles was a hole with a circle of tiny razor sharp teeth contracting open and closed. As he was drawn to the opening he shut his eyes.

Something kicked him. Opening his eyes he saw the blurry outline of Taymar, sword in hand, slicing the tentacles clear off. Sqwal shrieked in pain as its grip on Benjamin loosened. Taymar grabbed his elbow and they both headed towards the surface before a blow from Sqwal's tail sent them hurtling towards the cliff. Taymar motioned him forward as she kept slashing at Sqwal. Dark red blood floated in the water, following Benjamin as he reached the surface. He swam the few metres to the cliff face, the thrashing and groaning not far behind him. Finding small ledges and nooks, Benjamin started the slow climb up the rock face. As he looked down, it seemed that every side of Sqwal was different. He could see Taymar on top of an iceberg that Sqwal was pushing out to sea. She leapt from it and was on his back, surfing along as he thrashed about. The night was dark, lightened by the Northern Lights that swirled angrily above.

'Taymar!' Benjamin called twice, but he was too high up now, she couldn't hear him.

Nearing the top, he could hear snarls and growls in the distance. The cliff jutted out slightly above him, and he struggled to reach his arm over and pull himself up.

Then a gloved hand poked out from above him on the top of the point. Benjamin stumbled back, almost losing his footing, small chunks of rock sailing to the ocean below.

'Take my hand.'

Benjamin hung from the cliff for a moment, staring at the gloved hand. Attached to it a thick parka. There was a layer of snow around his cuffs.

'We don't have time, the wolves are coming,' the voice demanded. It wasn't a voice he recognised. Without another thought, Benjamin grabbed hold of the man's wrist. The man pulled Benjamin up with such force that his feet flung up through the air, landing on the ground a few feet from the cliff's edge.

He stood up and got his bearings. The same wolves that had attacked them in the tents were back. More of them this time, bigger and meaner, they were swarming the shore, waiting for Jeems who was on his way back to shore in the boat. Batar was with him, his body limp and lifeless. Batar was dead.

18

Saved. Stranded. Dead.

The man, dressed in a long tan parka, winter hat and snow goggles led Benjamin to his snowmachine. 'Get on.'

Benjamin took a step back.

'Look,' the man said, pointing down to the shore. 'Wolves. They're not coming for a tea party. This is your only chance to get out of here alive.'

'Who are you? I'm not leaving my friends.' Benjamin choked on the words, his bravery cheating him.

'Jeems and Taymar will be fine, they always are. It's you everyone is after. Now I'm not asking anymore. Get on!'

The sternness in the man's voice surprised Benjamin. He took one last look down below. Avoiding the wolves, Jeems had hauled Batar and the boat up on a flat piece of ice. He was cradling Batar with his good arm, crying and shouting something Benjamin couldn't hear. Taymar was swimming to Jeems, the water littered with what was left of Sqwal.

The snowmobile came to life, its motor ferocious in the crisp night air. Down below, the wolves by the shore howled and started heading towards them, joining the few others that were already half way across the point.

Pushing away guilt and remorse, Benjamin got on in front of the big man. With a jerk the snowmobile sped off. He didn't know where he was going or who he was with but he didn't care. Batar was dead, Marcus lied and Gideon was nowhere to be found. If Magh were right around the corner it wouldn't make for a worse day. The snowmobile picked up speed, the engine screamed. As if armoured, it threw the wolves to the side as they tried to jump and snap at Benjamin.

Regret found him. What if he was being taken to Magh? Then no one would know that Jericho is the traitor the exiles have been looking for. But, he reasoned, if he is going to Magh that wouldn't matter because Meridia was doomed either way.

Black outlines of snow and cliffs whizzed past them. Thoughts of Marcus crept back. Marcus. How could he have done this? Who is he? What is he? Anger gave way to exhaustion and Benjamin's head drooped, the sight of Jeems cradling Batar's limp body waiting for him every time he closed his eyes.

When Benjamin woke up they were driving through a forest, the morning sun was burning dull, slowly rising. The snowmobile was big but turned sharply through the thick trees. He noticed how cold he had become, a thick layer of snow crusted against the front of his parka. They drove up to the familiar waterfall and stopped.

'This is your stop,' the man broke the silence. 'Time to get off.'

Fighting under the weight of the crusted snow that had attached to his snow pants, Benjamin slowly got is leg over and slid off.

'Who are you?' He turned to the man.

But the man only started up his snowmobile again. 'Get inside,' he commanded over the engine's hum. 'Now.'

The man sat on his snowmachine, looking ahead, waiting for Benjamin to move. He finally mumbled thank you and turned to the entrance of Water's Hyde.

The warmth hit him the second he passed through. The fire was blazing, and the snow started to fall from him instantly. A bright ticking noise and then little Greyfriars ran to meet him, running across his cold snowy boots.

'Hey there, Greyfriars,' Benjamin chortled. 'Yeah, the snow is really cold. Just wait until I take some of this stuff off.'

His snow suit dripping at the entrance, Benjamin came through to the main room to where Gideon was sitting by the fire. Anger rose up in him and burned his cheeks.

'Who brought me here? And what about Jeems and Taymar? Are they dead too? Are they dead like Batar?' Unexpected tears streamed down his face. 'As long as you fill your precious Arcrux that's all that matters, that's all you care about.'

Greyfriars skulked away, her head down and tail between her legs. Benjamin stifled the urge to go to her softly and tell her he was sorry. But he wasn't sorry, he was angry, and he was finally able to let it out.

'Taymar and Jeems are bringing Batar's body back to Sasha where he belongs,' Gideon said quietly. He turned to look at Benjamin. 'Please sit down, you've had a long trip.'

Benjamin stood in front of Gideon. Sasha. Poor Sasha. He thought of how she fussed over them all before they left, how she insisted they test the tracking device for the sixth and seventh time.

'I'll stand thanks,' he said through clenched teeth. 'What about Sasha? What is she going to do now?'

'She will continue research, I'm sure. She will most likely go back to her people in Siberia.'

'So there are still people left? Not just the exiles?'

Gideon nodded.

'I don't get it!' Benjamin shouted. 'I don't get any of it. I think I do, then something totally random happens and I'm back at the beginning.' His eyes burned as he watched Gideon sitting in front of him. 'Are you just going to sit there? Are you just going to sit there and do nothing while people are dying?'

'I'm unsure, Benjamin, if you will be happy with any answer I give you at the moment.' Gideon's voice was calm. 'Your anger and sadness over Batar is understandable. Batar's death was tragic and unnecessary. A result of the mistakes made by men for generations.'

'So what, Batar has to pay for something that happened before he was even born?' Benjamin fought the urge to throw something.

'No,' Gideon said quietly. 'That would be unfair. People have been making choices since the

278

beginning of time. Choices that have, for the most part, led to pain, sickness and death. Therefore Magh has become the deputy of many soldiers. Soldiers of greed, gluttony, pride and anger. And that army creates chaos, fear and pain. Batar was in the army that is fighting her off, and that is why he was killed.'

'So it's no use, then? I've done this for nothing.'

'You are the one chance people have.' Gideon turned to face him. 'You are the last hope of shifting the balance. With you leading, the rest in Meridia will follow. Bit by bit, people outside of Meridia are being tested and tempted every day. Howl will never be happy until he has every living creature under his command, and so Magh and her army will do whatever they have to in order to do his bidding. So people must make choices everyday. Sometimes they choose well, sometimes they don't. It's all a part of the battle.'

Benjamin fell silent, thoughts and visions swirling through his head. His eyes rested on the scales that sat above the fireplace. Getting the league had made the scales shift again.

'You can see for yourself that what you are doing is making a difference,' Gideon pointed to the scales. 'You will sometimes have to choose to do things that are difficult merely because they are the right thing to do.'

He stood there for a long time, barely noticing Greyfriars twisting through his legs. Batar came to his mind, then Sasha. Tears blurred his vision. He clenched his teeth as his thoughts shifted to Marcus and the last coded note. Then thoughts kept coming, uncontrollable images. Jeems in the clearing, Sasha crying.

He turned to Gideon. 'Well, maybe I don't want to make a difference.' The voice was different. It was new – angry, shaky.

Without waiting for a reply, Benjamin strode towards the archway of the middle corridor. He kept his pace until he reached the door that would lead him back to Hadley Priest. He pushed back the voice in his head that was telling him to stop and strode on, taking the stairs two at a time.

He burst through the door to Hadley Priest. The morning sun was shining through the window, exposing the dust that had been stirred up from his entrance.

He closed the door and stood there for a minute, not really knowing what to do when he heard Hester's bedroom door open.

She looked at him for only a moment before her face twisted. 'Oh no you don't,' she shouted. 'I don't know how you got passed those locked doors, but you can get right back out! I told you if you ran away again you'd be out on the street, so get your coat and shoes on and get going.'

Woken by the commotion, Marcus and Riley came halfway down the stairs in their pyjamas. Marcus' curly hair high atop his head.

He gave them a sideways glance as he got his shoes on. 'Don't worry, I'm not staying. He strode out the front door and down the street without looking back.

19

A New Home

Benjamin walked until his feet could no longer carry him. By the busyness of the streets and shops, he guessed it was Saturday. Most of the Christmas decorations had been cleared out of their sale bins, giving a clue to how long after the holiday it was. Night fell early, which was welcome, as Benjamin was tired and starving. He managed to find some shelter under a foot bridge that covered a small river. He sat under the bridge, clutching his stomach and trying to forget everything that he had just been through, thankful to be drifting off to sleep.

'Benjamin. Benjamin, wake up,' he fought to open his heavy eyelids. He could feel someone nudging his shoulder, then memories flooded him again. He opened his eyes, ready to run. Marcus was crouched down next to him.

'I've been trying to find you for hours, it's really late. You've got to come back.'

Benjamin scrambled to his feet. 'Come back! To who? You? Why didn't you tell me you knew about Meridia? Who are you anyways?'

'I couldn't tell you, it was too risky,' Marcus pleaded, standing up.

'For who? You?'

'Not for me, for Riley you dim wit!' Do you think Motley would have just sat back if he knew? There would have been an all out war. As it is, he's been a nightmare -'

'Nightmare?' Benjamin interrupted. 'You want to talk about nightmares? I've had so many of them I could open a shop.'

'Right, okay I get it, I'm sorry. But it's not been easy out here. Mrs Wink's been on my case about you at school and -'

Benjamin didn't hear the rest. Mrs Wink – why hadn't he thought of her? She would help him.

'I don't care anymore,' Benjamin put his hand up to stop Marcus. 'You seem to know all about Meridia, you can take my place. I'm outta here.'

He stormed off at a run, not slowing down until he reached the Winks' house. The house was dark. He felt bad about waking them up but he was sure they would be happy to see him.

He looked up and down the street before going up the walkway to their door. His hand hovered over the knocker for a few seconds and then he rapped it hard.

A light switched on upstairs. Then footsteps coming downstairs. He started to shake with anticipation, his teeth chattering wildly. Another light now, this time in the entrance. He glimpsed at his reflection in the frosted glass. A few hours ago he was fighting wolves and a sea beast. He pushed it out of his mind.

Then the outline of a person. On the other side of the obscured glass was the unmistakable shape of Mrs Wink. A key in the door and then it opened a crack.

'Hi.' Benjamin hardly recognised his own voice.

'Benjamin?' Two weary brown eyes appeared in the crack of the doorway.

'Er – yeah, it's me.'

The rest of the door flung wide open. 'Oh my goodness! Are you alright? Where have you been? Your teeth are chattering, and you're shivering! Come in, you must be freezing.'

He let her usher him in. The house was warm and comfortable. He took off his coat as she locked the door behind him.

Lightning Source UK Ltd.
Milton Keynes UK
17 January 2011

165832UK00001B/18/P